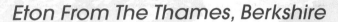

Eton From The Thames, Berkshire

TAKE a cruise along the majestic River Thames and you'll see some of London's most famous landmarks. The Tower of London, Houses of Parliament, the London Eye — London's familiar sights will be yours to survey from the river.

Then move on to Hampton Court Palace, still rumoured to be haunted by Henry VIII's fifth wife, Catherine Howard, running through the corridor begging to be allowed to see her husband.

Last stop on the tour is Windsor Castle — the largest inhabited castle in the world. Don't miss its dazzling State Apartments, world-famous paintings and chapel. There are also ten royal tombs here, including those of Henry VIII and Charles II.

D0997047

£5.70

People's Friend An

Dear Reader,

A warm welcome to the "Friend" Annual for 2004!

Inside you'll find 25 brand-new stories, by favourite "Friend" writers, to take you through the year season by season. We've got romance, humour, nostalgia — there's something here for everyone!

This year, we take a journey through the lives of the delightful couple on our cover in nine charming poems by Alice Drury. And we have our usual beautiful trip round Britain with J Campbell Kerr.

You can also enjoy a welcome glimpse of summer sun as we pay a visit to Britain's favourite holiday resorts of yesteryear!

So sit down, put your feet up and treat yourself to some time out with your favourite "Friend"!

Your Editor

Complete Stories

p28

J Campbell Kerr Paintings

p14

al 2004 Contents

p48

Their Life In Verse
by Alice Drury

p95

Famous Seaside Resorts

p24

5

HAPPY NEW YEAR!

"ENGAGED?" Maureen Slattery felt surprise and excitement rise within her at her son's unexpected news.

"Are you pleased?" Patrick asked, amusement laced with uncertainty in his voice.

"Of course, and your da will be thrilled. We just want you to be happy."

"I am. I know you've not met Nikki yet, but we'll be with you for New Year."

Maureen struggled to take all the information on board. Not only was her son engaged but, for the first time in his twenty-seven years, he would not be home for Christmas.

"I know it's a bit short

by Margaret McDonagh.

Illustration by John Hancock. 7

notice, but we weren't sure what we were doing. Now we plan to stop off for Christmas in Herefordshire with Nikki's family," Patrick confirmed, sounding less than pleased at the prospect, "and then come over to Ireland to spend some time with you. Is that OK?"

"Grand," Maureen agreed enthusiastically, burying her disappointment that they would be apart for the festive season.

Arrangements made, she hung up.

It was already December, but the weather had been kind, a warm autumn giving way gently to the idea of the winter to come. Crisp mornings, often veiled in gentle mists over the Wicklow hills, had preceded shortening days of weak sunshine.

So far there had been little rain, and Kevin had been able to get many of the frustrating jobs finished off round the farm.

He was out there now, doing the milking, and would soon be in for his tea. Setting the kettle on the range, Maureen looked out of the window at the gathering dusk, and wondered what the house would feel like over the holiday with just the two of them.

This was a time of year she always looked forward to, knowing that Patrick would be coming home. They so seldom saw him now he was a successful doctor in a hospital in England.

I T was what they wanted for him, of course. Whatever disappointment Kevin had harboured at his son's lack of interest in the farm had long since been overcome by his pride in Patrick's achievements.

Maureen, bursting with pride herself, would have preferred him to stay this side of the water and take his training in Ireland, but he had needed to spread his wings. She understood that. But she missed him.

The back door clattered and Kevin came in, kicking off his boots and padding across the stone-flagged floor to his warm slippers by the range.

"The tea is just on." Maureen smiled.

Kevin dropped a kiss on her forehead.

"The very thing, love, thanks."

"Patrick rang," Maureen informed him as she set steaming mugs of tea on the table and cut her husband a generous slice of fruit cake.

"And he's well?"

"He's fine." Stirring a teaspoon of sugar into her tea, Maureen sighed. "He had one or two bits of news."

"Indeed?"

"He's engaged, don't you know!"

"Is he now?" Kevin grinned broadly. "And who is she?"

"A girl called Nikki. I think she's a teacher. But he's not said a lot about her, not even in his letters," Maureen admitted, a frown creasing her brow. "Still, he sounds very happy."

"That's the main thing. And is he bringing her for Christmas?"

Sighing again, Maureen's frown deepened.

"No, for New Year. Apparently they're stopping at her family's for Christmas on their way here."

Disappointment flickered in Kevin's blue eyes before he rallied.

"Ah, well, that's the way of things, I suppose."

"Yes."

"Come on, love," he cajoled her with an understanding smile, taking her hand and giving it a reassuring squeeze. "It had to happen some time. We've been luckier than most."

Maureen smiled back.

"You're right. We'll have a good Christmas, won't we, and be ready for an extra-special New Year?"

DESPITE her determination to make the best of their first Christmas alone, Maureen found it hard.

Besides the daily round of routine work, there was much to do, seeing friends, attending church and village activities, entertaining assorted cousins. But the sense of something — someone — missing was an ever-present ache that nagged at her.

Maureen acknowledged that one of the reasons was her sadness that Patrick had been an only child. How she would have loved a house full of youngsters, but it was not to be.

She had been blessed with Patrick, and was thankful for him always, but the regret that no big family had followed was deep-seated.

How lovely it would have been now, she thought, with Patrick away, to have had other family, maybe even grandchildren, taking the silence from the rambling old farmhouse.

She and Kevin spent a quiet time, leaving the presents at the foot of the tree to enjoy when Patrick and Nikki came. They enjoyed being together, but each was counting the days until the New Year.

"I wonder what Nikki is like?" Maureen wondered aloud as she sat down with Kevin for a hearty breakfast after morning milking on the last day of the year.

"If she's the one for Patrick, I'm sure she'll be grand," he replied, helping himself to more scrambled egg. "Must be something of an ordeal for her, having to meet the family — same as for Patrick, spending Christmas with hers."

"I hadn't thought of that," Maureen admitted, determining at once to make sure the girl felt at ease.

Kevin smiled.

"Still, when you think of some of the lasses he brought home as a teenager!"

9

"Oh, don't! One or two were very strange, weren't they?"

"A varied collection of way-out clothes and scary hairdos!" Finishing his breakfast, Kevin rose to his feet. "Don't you be worrying now, love. I'll be working around the barn so I'll hear the car when it comes."

Maureen watched him cross the yard, her heart as full of love for him as when they had married thirty years before. He was a good man, dependable, loyal, caring. She hoped her son would be as good a husband to Nikki as Kevin had been to her.

I T was late morning when Maureen heard a car arriving outside. She'd made up the spare beds, had lunch all prepared, and now she dried her hands, tidied her hair and, ignoring the flutter of nerves in the pit of her stomach, hurried outside to greet the arrivals.

The last days of rain had given way to weak sunshine, bathing the stunning scenery in a gentle mellowness. It was cold, and her breath misted the air as she walked across to the car.

Already Patrick was out from behind the wheel, embracing his father. He turned to her, seeming taller and broader than when he had been home last, briefly at Easter, his dark hair thick and trimmed, his bright eyes, so like his father's, glowing with inner happiness.

"It's grand to see you!" she greeted him, hugging him back as tightly as he was hugging her.

"You, too, Mam. It's great to be home." He stepped back, smiling, and held out a hand to the young woman who came round the car to join them. "I want you to meet Nikki Palmer, my fiancée!"

Maureen smiled, holding out her arms and welcoming the girl with a friendly embrace, noticing her shyness and anxiety.

"It's grand to meet you, love."

"Indeed." Kevin grinned, shaking Nikki's hand warmly.

"Come away inside now, where it's warm," Maureen insisted. "I've the kettle on and I expect you'll be glad of something after your journey."

Nikki smiled.

"Thank you."

"Da and I will bring the bags," Patrick suggested.

In the homely, rustic kitchen, Maureen made the coffee, allowing herself a first study of the girl who was to be her daughter-in-law. Of medium height, Nikki had pretty blonde hair and warm hazel eyes.

She was casually dressed in comfortable trousers and a pale pink shirt, and she wore the barest minimum of make-up to accentuate her long-lashed eyes.

"Please, do sit down and make yourself at home." Maureen gestured to a chair, eager that Nikki feel comfortable. "Was it a rough crossing?"

"A bit. I'm not the best of sea travellers, I'm afraid," Nikki admitted.

10

The Meeting

KATE and Joe remember well
The day when first they met.
That day would shape their futures
Though they didn't know it yet.

Kate was only six years old,
And Joe just two years more,
When he and all his family
Arrived to live next door.

They soon became the best of friends
And played in harmony;
Taking turns to push the swing
Upon the apple tree.

It was a blissful childhood
For this happy little pair;
Each knowing that, not far away,
The other one was there.

– Alice Drury.

Maureen smiled back.

"Just the thought of the ferry and I'm green around the gills!"

Kevin and Patrick, the bags stowed upstairs, joined them round the table, and Maureen was glad to see that Nikki soon lost her nervous shyness.

* * * *

It was a happy reunion and they lingered over their meal before Kevin announced he had to attend to the stock.

"I'll come and help you," Patrick offered.

Pulling on his boots, Kevin smiled.

"Think you still have it in you?" he teased.

After they had gone, Nikki insisted on helping clear away, and then Maureen showed her upstairs.

"I hope you'll be comfy here," she worried. "Patrick will be just next door and the bathroom is straight across the landing."

"Thank you, it's lovely."

"Anything you need, please ask."

"I will." Nikki turned from admiring the view from the window and smiled. "You've made me so welcome."

IMPULSIVELY Maureen hugged her, sensing some inner conflict the girl was trying to hide.

"Is everything all right, love?"

"Yes, fine. I — well, I just wish my own family were as accepting as you," she admitted, biting her lip as if wishing she hadn't said so much.

"I see."

"It's not that they don't like Patrick himself," Nikki continued, "but they have never approved of what I wanted to do with my life."

"But it's your life to do with as you wish."

Nikki smiled at that.

"Yes, but they had grand plans for their daughter to follow in the family footsteps as my two older brothers have done. I'm not very popular because I broke the mould and followed my own dreams.

"I think they even had a husband picked out for me, someone I have known all my life, the son of my father's business partner. But —"

"But you don't love him," Maureen finished for her, sitting on the bed.

Nikki sat down, too.

"No, not at all. But I love Patrick so very much. I've never felt like this about anyone in my life."

"Then you must follow your own heart," Maureen advised, slipping an arm comfortingly around the girl's shoulders. "I'm sure your family will come round when they see how happy you are."

"I hope so. Thank you for listening."

"Any time." She rose to her feet and held out her hand. "Come with me, Nikki. I want to show you something."

She led her future daughter-in-law to the adjacent room that had been Patrick's all his life at home. Looking round, she smiled reminiscently.

"I can still see how it was when Patrick was a boy, littered with abandoned toys, books and clothes!

"He was an adventurous child, always outside, always in some mischief with his friends, falling in streams, arriving home grubby and with his clothes torn. And his pockets were always bulging with conkers and odd bits of string and sticky, half-sucked toffees!"

Nikki laughed, clearly delighted at these insights of Patrick as a boy. "What else?"

"He had his Thunderbirds phase," Maureen remembered, shaking her head at the memories. "He'd roar round the house yelling at the top of his voice and answering FAB to everything anyone said to him!

"Then there was football, followed by music — always at full volume, which drove his da and me mad!"

MAUREEN sobered, thinking how they had missed that noise since Patrick had left for the London teaching hospital.

"He's always spoken of his childhood here with such affection and love," Nikki said. "Did he never want to take on the farm?"

"No. He just wasn't interested. His da was always sorry about that, but our son had his own dreams and ambitions, and it was important that he follow them."

Nikki nodded, relating the ideas to her own situation.

"And is Mr Slattery still sorry?"

"Kevin, or Da!" Maureen corrected gently. "No, love. I can assure you that no man could be prouder of his son than Kevin is of Patrick. He's a fine young man, as I'm sure you know, and however hard it is for parents to see their young fly the nest, you learn to let go."

"You must miss him."

"Ah, of course I do! That's what mothers are for, to fret and worry over their offspring! And I'd have loved more," she admitted now, voicing aloud her secret regret. "But there we go."

Smiling, Nikki hugged her with fresh warmth and spontaneity.

"That's what I want, too. A house full of children of my own. Your grandchildren."

"I'd like nothing better."

Forcing back a sudden sting of tears, Maureen rubbed her hands briskly together.

"Well, this won't get the chores done!"

DRUMMOND CASTLE, PERTHSHIRE: J CAMPBELL KERR.

"Thank you . . . for everything."

"You're welcome." She laid a hand against Nikki's soft cheek. "Just come down when you're ready, love."

The rest of the day passed happily, and during the evening they opened the presents they had saved from Christmas, keeping out the evening chill with a roaring log fire in the cosy sitting-room, and sipping the special whiskey Patrick had brought for his father.

As midnight approached, they gathered round the old clock, their glasses ready, and counted down the chimes to the New Year, smiling and hugging as the hour struck.

"Well, I must away to my bed or the cows will not be milked in the morning!" Kevin laughed.

"Before you go, Da, Nikki and I have something we'd like to tell you both."

MAUREEN felt a strange sense of unease settle inside her and wondered what this latest piece of news was. She hoped they weren't going to say they were marrying on some exotic beach and depriving her of a grand wedding, or emigrating to Australia.

"We wanted to wait until the stroke of New Year to tell you." Nikki smiled. "But it was so hard keeping it to myself earlier!"

Patrick took Nikki's hand in his.

"We've done a lot of talking about our future, what we want for us and, hopefully, for our soon-to-be family. You've always supported me in everything I have ever done, and the life I've had here was the best. Thank you both for all you have given me."

"It's been our pleasure, son." Maureen was gratified.

Drummond Castle, Perthshire

DRUMMOND CASTLE consists of an old keep, now used as a museum, and a modern wing built early in the 19th century.

The gardens at Drummond are one of the showpieces of the county. The original garden was laid out by John, 2nd Earl of Perth, in the 17th century. In 1840 a more elaborate plan was completed, centred on a sundial that tells what the time is in all the principal cities of Europe.

The gardens contain many rare trees and shrubs and are open to visitors at stated times during the summer. If you're a gardener yourself, you won't want to miss this rare treat!

"We've always wanted what was best for you," Kevin added in agreement. "And no-one could be more proud of you."

"As I am of you. Anyway," Patrick continued, clearing his throat, "Nikki and I hope to marry at Easter, as you know, and we were hoping that maybe we could be married in Ireland."

"Oh, that would be grand!" Maureen responded happily.

"It's what we both want," Nikki agreed.

"The thing is," Patrick went on, "that we have both decided to make some changes at work, too. Nikki has her heart set on a big family and plans to spend as much time at home as she can, working part-time when she wants to — although her family think her very unambitious and old-fashioned.

"As for me," he added with a mischievous grin of old, "I've been offered a job in Dublin. I've accepted it."

IT took a moment for his words to sink in. Maureen put a hand to her throat, hardly daring to believe it was true.

"You're coming home?" she whispered.

"Yes, Mam. A New Year with new beginnings for us all. What do you think?"

Laughing through her tears, Maureen hugged her son and his future wife.

"I think it is the greatest gift you could have given your da and me!"

"Thanks to both of you," Kevin toasted, his own eyes glistening with happiness.

After the others had gone happily to their beds, Maureen lingered alone in the homely warmth of the kitchen. Just weeks ago she had been worrying at the first of many Christmases that lay ahead for herself and Kevin on their own and wondering what might have been.

Now, she felt that not only had she gained Nikki as Patrick's soon-to-be-bride, but as a friend, an honorary daughter, and generous-spirited, perfect mother for a horde of grandchildren.

Listening to the quiet sounds of the house settling down for sleep, she smiled to herself, imagining in years to come the fresh noise of children scampering through its corridors, filling it with joy and love, at Christmas and throughout the year.

How lucky she was! How blessed. The son who had stretched his wings and flown free was coming home to roost with the woman he loved.

It was indeed a New Year . . . a time for new beginnings, new hope and a happy new future for them all. ■

NEXT Saturday should be one of the happiest days of my life — but all I can do is think of Bill, and of how much he would have wanted to be here, to walk Claire down the aisle, his arm in hers.

I try to keep smiling, for Claire's sake, but it's so hard. With all the wedding arrangements — caterers, photographers, the dress — I can't help thinking back to mine and Bill's big day.

I remember it as clearly as if it was just last week. The sun was shining, there wasn't a cloud in the sky, and I could see my whole future ahead of me. My future with Bill.

But now I'm on my own, and the future holds nothing but uncertainty.

The groom-to-be, bridesmaids, best man, my brother, Colin, my sister, Marjorie, and myself are sitting at the front of the church with the vicar. We're all here apart from Claire, the bride. The rehearsal was meant to begin at one o'clock; it's now half-past.

Light pours through the stained-glass

When The Time Is Right

by Alison Burton.

Illustration by Melvyn Warren-Smith.

windows, creating colourful mosaics on the dark wood and red carpet.

After a few more minutes the doors burst open and Claire tumbles in, full of apologies.

"Hi, everyone. Sorry I'm late. Hi, Mum."

I stand up and give her a hug.

"Hi, love. I wondered if you were having second thoughts for a minute."

"No way." She gazes at Chris. "This one's for keeps."

The vicar begins to talk and everyone listens, apart from me. I've heard his words before.

Laughter suddenly echoes to the rafters. I didn't hear the joke, but the sound distracts me from my thoughts and I turn around.

Claire and Colin are practising the timing of their steps. They have to return to the start when Colin treads on her foot. Claire's wearing that big smile of hers, the one that means everything is perfect.

I want to be pleased that she's happy, but all I can think is that it's Colin walking by her side, not Bill. How can she smile that smile when everything is far from perfect?

WHEN Bill died two months ago, Claire was quiet for a while. I found it hard to hold back the tears, so she'd sit there at the kitchen table, her hand resting on mine, murmuring the soothing words I should have been saying to her.

I tried getting her to talk about how she felt, but she always managed to switch it back to me, or change the subject completely.

I've often wondered if she misses her father much at all . . .

The vicar takes everybody to the back of the church and shows us the wedding register room. It's still the cramped little space I remember.

We return to the main part of the church and, after a few more details, the vicar reads out the order people will leave in. Claire and Chris will go first, through the archway entrance that so many couples have passed through before. The same one Bill and I went through all those years ago.

I didn't only lose my husband when Bill died, but all my dreams as well. Because they weren't just my dreams, they were ours. We'd booked a trip of a lifetime for this month; we'd have been flying overseas in a fortnight's time.

It was something we'd always wanted to do, and we'd worked hard and saved hard, going without a few things until we had the money. The journey would have started in the Far East before going on to China, India and Egypt. The tickets are still at home, tucked away in a drawer, all but forgotten.

After saying goodbye to everyone, my sister, Marjorie, and I chat about different weather forecasts for the weekend and what colour she should wear so we don't clash in the photos.

About fifteen minutes later we wander out into the bright winter sunlight. I head for my car, about to leave for home, but then turn back. I decide to visit Bill; his ashes were scattered in the Garden of Rest here.

I T'S peaceful as I round the corner of the church and, in spite of the snow, the sun feels warm on my face as I open the small gate leading to the garden. Bill's memorial stone is in a corner, under an oak tree. But as I approach, the sound of a familiar voice stops me short.

"Oh, Dad, how I wish you could be here."

Claire's facing the stone, with her back towards me.

"You don't know how much I want you to give me away, it just won't be the same with Uncle Colin . . ." She pauses. "And Mum's been acting very strangely."

I lean a bit closer.

"Of course, she must still be upset, but she doesn't seem to realise that I'm hurting just as much. Just because I don't cry all the time doesn't mean I don't miss you. I miss you more than anything in the world.

"It's just . . . and I hate to admit this, but I think Mum and I . . . we're drifting apart. I've already lost you; I don't want to lose Mum as well."

That's it. I can't hold back any longer.

"Claire!" I emerge from my hiding place and kneel down to hug her.

"Mum?"

"I'm sorry I've been so selfish. I should have known that you were hurting, too."

"It's OK, Mum."

A few moments pass and I wonder who's supporting who. Finally, Claire breaks away and wipes her eyes, embarrassed.

"I'd better go and tell Chris where I am — I'll be back in a minute."

She runs up the little path and when she gets to the gate she turns around and waves.

I smile as she disappears from sight, then glance up. The sun is still shining and there isn't a cloud in the sky. All of a sudden, I realise the uncertainty of the future doesn't matter.

No-one knows for sure what tomorrow will bring, or what bridges they'll have to cross. It's part of life.

I look at the marble stone in front of me and, for the first time since Bill died, I know that, some day, I'll take that trip around the world. It won't be in two weeks, and it probably won't be next year, but I know I will do it.

And what's more, I won't be crying into a tissue when I get on the plane. I'll be looking up into the sky and smiling a big smile like Claire's; because everything will be perfect . . . ■

Her Secret

BRENDA had been keeping a secret for fifty-one years. It wasn't a deadly serious secret, or one that she was deliberately hiding from anybody; it wasn't even something she thought about much. Once a year, perhaps — if that.

And — here was the thing — she might never have thought of it again, if it hadn't fallen out of a newspaper while she was sorting through some old clothes and stuff in the attic.

It lay at the bottom of the tea chest and, when she saw it, her heart registered a single, gentle thud of recognition.

She reached into the chest and, as she did so, the sight of her hand in the torchlight gave her a jolt. It was as if she were looking at a stranger's skin, embossed with veins, and aged by years she'd no memory of.

The feeling subsided in a moment, but it left her thinking about the passing of time and the woman

by John Heyes.

she had become. She smiled to herself. Oh, Brenda, you're a giddy old fool, she thought, bringing the card up close and running her fingers gently over its lettering.

It had dropped on to the mat in her house on the morning of St Valentine's Day, 1951. Her mother, scurrying about in that brief gap between Dad going to work and the kids getting up, had found and opened it, even though the envelope was clearly addressed to *Miss Brenda Thomas*.

Valentine

Brenda could still see her mother waving the envelope angrily in the air.

"You know what your dad would say if he saw this, don't you?"

Brenda had said nothing. Her mother wasn't in the best of moods, and she'd been sick again that morning.

"I've a good mind to burn it, put paid to all those romantic notions in your head once and for all."

B RENDA had learned over the years not to answer back to her mother — it usually only made her even angrier. She lowered her eyes and waited.

"Take it," her mother said finally.

Brenda grabbed the envelope from her outstretched hand and ran back upstairs with it as fast as she could

* * * *

Even now, fifty years later, Brenda Thomas-as-was could still recall

Illustration by Graham Williams.

21

how she'd felt when opening the card for the first time:

Roses are red
Leaves are so green
You are the prettiest
Girl I have seen.

No signature, no romantic nom de plume. In classic secret admirer style, there was no clue as to the identity of her mystery swain.

But here was proof someone had once regarded her as not only pretty, but prettier even than Susan Bell or Anna Hinchcliffe. Those two were invariably turned out well and always seemed to look down on Brenda and her friend, Sandra.

Of course, Brenda made sure they got to know about her card. Their faces were a picture when they "accidentally" saw her showing it to Sandra!

That morning she'd sat on the bed to look at her reflection in the dressing-table mirror. Before her was a tall girl with blue eyes, whose fair hair shone under the bare light bulb. Her lips were red and the blush of embarrassment in her cheeks gave the skin a delicate rouge colour . . .

It was as if she'd been given permission to see herself in a more flattering light. As she'd stood up and looked out of the window over the frame of the dresser mirror, the morning sun had flowed like a flood along the cobbled street.

With it came a sense of the whole world opening up to her. Brenda had fancied she lived not in grimy old Horton but in a smart flat in some seaside town like Scarborough. The sea was just over there, behind the gas cylinder . . .

"WHO sent it, then?" her mother asked as Brenda floated down to breakfast.

"How would I know?"

"I bet you do know." Her mother sniffed. "You'd better not let your dad find out, though, that's all I'm telling you."

"I've hidden it. Don't worry."

The heavy silence was broken only by the ticking of the clock in the corner. Mam dished out the porridge then pierced a slice of bread and dangled it above the glowing coals of the fire.

"You've got no idea, really?" she said, taking her attention off the smoking bread for a moment.

"No, Mam, honestly."

"I saw him, you see. The lad who delivered it."

Brenda's pulse fluttered. She took a sip of tea while she settled her thoughts.

"Looked a nice lad," her mother said, scraping some dripping on the toast. "I only saw him from the back, like."

Brenda let her spoon sink back into the bowl. From above came the noise of her brothers getting up.

"Better get them ready," her mother said briskly. "It's all go in here this morning."

How tall was he? Did he have sticky-out ears? What was he wearing? Brenda would have to ask — in a roundabout way, though, when she could think of one. She didn't want her mam to think she was too interested.

She pushed back her chair and sloped off towards the hallway.

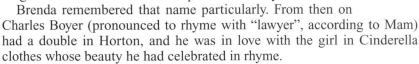

"A bit of a posh young chap, he looked," her mother called out as Brenda reached the door. "Nice long black coat. White scarf. Proper Charles Boyer."

Brenda remembered that name particularly. From then on Charles Boyer (pronounced to rhyme with "lawyer", according to Mam) had a double in Horton, and he was in love with the girl in Cinderella clothes whose beauty he had celebrated in rhyme.

AND that was all she knew, or ever learned, about her secret admirer. For days, going into weeks, Brenda had measured every lad she saw against the romantic template of her mother's description. None, however, quite matched the image her imagination had conjured up.

Of course, there were candidates — three in particular, if she was honest.

First to mind was Alan Richardson. His dad owned the paper shop at the top of the street. He was a nice lad. No Charles Boyer, though.

He had asked her to a dance once, at Christmas. The trouble was, he had a habit of wiping his nose on his sleeve, and at her age, things like that put you off easily.

Actually, she thought, looking back, it still would. But Alan had changed over the years. He'd inherited his dad's business, and now he owned Richardson's, the biggest newsagent's in Yorkshire, and had shops all over the place.

Brenda seldom saw him now, the last time being on Barnsley high street. He'd looked as if he recognised her, but she couldn't be sure.

Then there'd been Nigel Dander, the fat bully from across the street. He was the kind of lad others didn't stare at, even

Affectionately known as the "Queen" of seaside resorts, Bournemouth faces south, has a mild climate and a beach which boasts six miles of golden sand. Palm trees scatter the landscape and even line some streets, and the steeply rising cliffs provide a magnificent background to the Esplanade.

Bournemouth has wide streets, a pier, a pavilion, a theatre and its own symphony orchestra.

It's extremely busy in the summer, thanks to foreign tourists and British nationals alike, and the temperatures can sometimes make you feel as if you're basking in the Mediterranean sun!

when they felt his eyes heavy on them, daring them to.

He never bullied her, though. In fact, he'd saved her from being hurt in junior school, when a lad called Bruce Clark daily pinned her against the wall to demand sweets she hadn't got.

Brenda had had a soft spot for Nigel after he'd given Bruce Clark a talking-to, but there was never anything more to it than gratitude.

Nigel had stopped talking to her after she refused to partner him on a fancy-dress dray at the gala the following June. He'd gone, dressed as a caveman, because he couldn't afford a costume. It suited him. Eventually he'd forgiven her, and now when they passed in the street he'd give her a tight-lipped smile.

After leaving school, Nigel had got a job and raised a large, happy-looking family. His grandchildren loved him dearly and he had turned out a better man than most people had thought he would.

THE third contender was Jeffrey Dale. Brenda had been best friends with his sister Sandra for years and years.

Jeffrey was a funny lad, mad on gangster films and cowboys, calling other lads "brother" and "buddy" — a comical thing for a fifteen-year-old, just starting down the pit. He was always in the background when Brenda sat in their front room waiting for Sandra to get ready for

© *Pictor International.*

their weekly outing to the Chapel club.

The club was the only place her dad would let her go to after six at night. There they sang hymns she hardly knew and talked about Jesus, in between listening to the preacher's unmemorable sermons.

However boring it was, though, there was one really good thing about it — it wasn't home. The stern faces of the preacher and the piano player, Mrs Tong — a tall, large-boned lady with a gammy leg — were the visages of angels when compared to Brenda's dad in florid-faced, after-work short temper.

Sandra, as the only girl in her household, saw the club as a sanctuary, too. She suffered daily from a lack of privacy and the incessant teasing of her four brothers.

"The only time our Jeff doesn't get on at me," she told Brenda, "is when you turn up. I think he's soft on you. You'd be mad to go out with him, though. His feet smell something awful!"

That was her trio of admirers, one of whom had probably sent the card.

25

All right, none of them was perfect, but at seventeen, perfect was what she had been looking for.

Not now, of course — the years had forced some wisdom into her head along with the wrinkles they'd pressed on her brow. And maturity had changed every one of those potential suitors, too. Even Jeffrey, who now, according to Sandra, ran a caterers' firm supplying ocean liners.

Brenda had no idea where that talent had come from, but people constantly surprised you in life. Either that or they disappointed you, and you shouldn't blame them for that.

Which set her off thinking about Len again . . .

LEN, the man she'd married, the father of Jane, Anna and Betty, had come into her life later in the same year she'd got the card. Len was working on the same shift as her dad, and the two of them would walk home together from the pit. Brenda met them one day, on an errand for her mam.

Dad's companion, slighter and obviously younger than him, was covered in coal dust and shiny eyed, with teeth that glowed. Brenda hadn't a clue what he really looked like under all that grime.

Len began calling for her dad soon after, on his way to work. Not a handsome lad, he was attractive in a relaxed, easy-going sort of way. In fact, it was his attitude she liked most. Whereas all the other lads were not quite grown up, Len exuded a calm and self-containment that made him seem a lot older than them.

Her father liked him, too, and that was so unusual it added to his charm.

At nineteen years old, Len Baker was a finished product, a lad with a quip for all occasions.

"I don't like days, can't stand nights, and I'm not struck on afters," he said once on the subject of the pit.

"He's been engaged more times than the high street toilet," was another memorable remark he came up with when a particularly amorous workmate announced his latest attachment.

It was hard not to like Len, and harder still, when he finally proposed, to refuse. On top of everything else, her mother needed the room to house the rapidly-expanding family. In the end Brenda had fourteen siblings. How did her poor mother cope?

Life with Len had its ups and downs, of course, but out of it had come three lovely girls and five grandchildren, and she doted on them all.

Once in a long while, Brenda wished she had more romance in her life, that Len would show his feelings more; but maybe that was just the seventeen-year-old in her who still hankered after perfection.

This Valentine card was the only one Brenda had ever received. It was precious, both as a memento of the past, and of lost possibilities. And yes, on certain, rare occasions she'd find herself wondering — what if? What if she had married the one who had sent it?

Len's sense of humour, she had come to realise, was a mask behind which he hid his feelings. His childhood had been hard; his father died in the war, and his mother married a man who had little time for her former husband's children. Len went to lodge with old Pardoe the rag and bone man when he was just fifteen.

He and Brenda had come from unhappy backgrounds, and had clung together to make a new go at life. And in so many ways they had succeeded.

Len, God bless him, was gone now. That was why she was here, in the attic without a light bulb, sorting through the souvenirs of her marriage. To think her husband had never seen the card gave her a feeling of relief; to think she'd actually saved it all these years, a little guilt. It wasn't a secret she'd ever intended to keep, it had just happened that way.

SHE sighed, put down the card and piled all the other things back in the chest. Then a thought occurred to her.

She took them all out again and dug out the newspaper the card had fallen from. Something about it didn't make sense.

It was easy to imagine how the card had survived all these years. She must have brought it with her when she got married, along with all her other personal possessions.

So how come the newspaper it had been in was less than five years old?

Curious, she took it on to the landing and spread it out on the floorboards. There was a picture of a young girl picking up her BA, an advert for Richardson's, and a feature called "Pictures From The Past".

Well, well, she thought, reading from the top of the page.

Mrs Susan Dale, nee Bell, sends us this delightful photograph taken at the town gala, June, 1951. Susan herself, along with her friend, Anna Hinchcliffe, rides on the fancy dress dray as Scarlett O'Hara. Relatives and friends may notice Mr Nigel Dander, who married Miss Hinchcliffe, as the caveman in the centre. The dray was loaned for use by local rag and bone merchant Sam Pardoe, whose name can just be seen below the valance . . .

But Brenda had stopped reading. There, at the front of the cart, reins in hand, was the driver. He wore a long, black coat, a white scarf, and a huge top hat. Grainy though the print was, to Brenda's absolute delight, there was no mistaking Len's smiling face atop the brilliant white scarf. ■

Illustration by Mark Viney.

The Best-lo

I LOVE her. Really, I do. I'm just not very good at showing it. And Emma's the sort who loves romantic gestures. She'd be right at home in a slushy novel, and I've a sneaking feeling that the guy from those old Milk Tray adverts is pretty close to her ideal man.

But all she'd got was me. Assuming, of course, that she still wanted me. After last night, I wasn't sure about that.

"You don't have a romantic bone in your body!" she'd yelled when I'd rejected a cosy evening in in favour of the football. "I bet you don't even know

by Tia Brown.

when Valentine's Day is, do you?"

"February the fourteenth," I said, but the smug smile died on my lips when I realised that was the day after tomorrow.

"And you haven't organised anything, have you?" she went on with gloomy relish, and I knew it was now or never.

"Of course I have."

Oh, it was sweet to see her expression. Doubt, surprise, maybe even a little guilt that she might have misjudged me.

"Why didn't you tell me before?"

"It wouldn't be a surprise then, would it?"

She loves surprises, and I know I don't provide them often enough. But she gave me the benefit of the doubt, and hugged me.

I enjoyed the embrace, and began to

d Plans . . .

feel worried. I wanted to make this right for her sake, but I had a feeling that it wasn't going to be that simple.

This morning, after an hour on the phone ringing everything from the romantic little Italian restaurant on the high street to, in desperation, the Indian restaurant she hates, I knew what the word worried really meant. I mightn't be Milk Tray Man material, but I knew that Valentine's Day ought to mean romance.

And romance means meals — expensive meals, with soft lights and sweet music. She's allergic to flowers and she hates cuddly animals, but she's the chocoholic to end all chocoholics. But ordinary chocs won't do for my Emma. She's into continental chocolates; the sort you need a second mortgage for if you're going to buy more than a quarter of a pound.

Still, it wasn't as if I was going to be spending too much on the meal, the way things were going, so I bit the bullet and bought a beautiful ribbon-wrapped box.

I found a really good card, too, so if I'd only kept my mouth shut about that stupid surprise I'd definitely have been in her good books.

WORK'S never been what I'd call engrossing at the best of times. Today definitely wasn't that, so I resorted to staring out of the window instead. There were seagulls perching on top of the tall lampposts. Lucky them. They didn't have to worry about celebrations designed to make florists and restaurant owners wealthy. They flew wild and free under the starlight.

Now that wasn't such a bad idea. Starlight had to count as romantic in anyone's book. I could make a winter picnic — the weather was mild enough.

Fired by enthusiasm, and a smug feeling that this romance business was much easier than I'd realised, I swung into action after work. A trip round the supermarket took care of most of it, and a couple of tartan rugs and a waterproof ground sheet completed my plans. All I had to do was drop the right sort of hints.

Just her, me and the starlight. Oh, and that little box I bought from the jeweller's that's been sitting in my pocket for weeks, waiting for the right moment.

I rang her that evening.

"About tomorrow night," I began hesitantly.

"It's all right." Emma's voice was warm with laughter, rich with love, edged with a dispiriting tolerance. "I know we're not going out."

"We are going out," I said, before my worse nature let me grab the get-out clause with both hands. "But it isn't a conventional evening. Wrap up warm."

I'll admit I was nervous. But what better night was there to ask a girl to marry you? What better place than the hilltop where we met? She was walking her gran's dog. I was teaching my nephew to fly a kite. The rest is history.

HI," I said as she opened the door.
"Where are we going?" She greeted me in her own wonderful way, and I smiled enigmatically.
"Somewhere romantic. I'd put my wellies on if I were you."

She didn't answer that, and her smile was a bit worrying, but who cared? Tonight I was going to show her I could be as romantic as any man she'd ever dreamed of. I'd even cleaned the car, and the heater had been running so it was nice and warm.

"Oh, Mark," she said, when she realised where we were going.

"You like the idea? I've brought rugs, and there's a flask of soup, and little nibbly things and, well . . ." No wonder the Milk Tray Man went to such lengths to avoid speaking to the woman of his dreams. He probably couldn't think of anything to say, either!

Her gloved hand slipped into mine as we walked up the hill, and I was so happy that my throat sort of choked up. It was as romantic as any slushy novelist could have wished for.

The stars were bright, the hill was quiet, that jewellery box in my pocket was growing steadily heavier, and I knew exactly what I was going to say. Best of all, she was enjoying it. We might have been cold, but we were together. No distractions, no thoughts about all the things we ought to do. Just us.

"Emma." I cleared my throat, reached into my pocket, and then the heavens opened.

I don't mean a polite shower. I mean a downpour. We scrambled to stuff things back into the hamper, covered our heads with the ground sheet and scampered back down the hill, laughing like crazy kids.

"I'm sorry," I gasped as I dumped the stuff in the car boot, and we dived into the car.

"Only you!" She was still laughing and, even with her mascara running, she was more beautiful than any girl has a right to be. "Only you could do something like this, Mark. I love you."

She flung her arms around me and kissed me; and then it was easy.

"I love you, too, Emma. Will you marry me?"

That was all that needed to be said. She cried a bit, and hugged me quite a lot and everything was perfect. Except for one small problem — she sat on those horrendously expensive chocolates! But neither of us cared. After all, the Milk Tray Man never even got a kiss; and I bet he won't live as happily ever after as I'm going to! ■

IT was Gran's fault, really. If I hadn't been feeling particularly low at the time, I wouldn't have dreamed of taking notice of an old superstition!

But there I was, in Gran's cosy kitchen, pouring out my woes about boyfriends, or rather, lack of them, and actually considering her suggestion.

"'Hares' tonight, Lucy," Gran said firmly. "And 'rabbits' tomorrow."

I sipped my tea and pondered the idea.

"How on earth can saying 'hares' and 'rabbits' change my life? Do you really believe in this superstition, Gran?"

"Of course!" Gran's knitting needles clacked. "When I was a girl I went out of March on 'hares' and into April on 'rabbits'. Good things always happened afterwards!"

"But what happens if I say 'hares', and the phone rings before I'm asleep?"

"Then you speak to whoever's calling, say 'hares' again and settle down."

"What if I forget to say 'rabbits' when I wake up?"

"Then you'll have to wait until next year for that special luck."

I studied Gran's smiling face. True, she always seemed to be a

by Fay Wentworth.

Lucky For Some!

very happy person, but I could hardly attribute that to the fact that she said "hares" and "rabbits" as March slid into April!

Imagine if anyone heard! I could just picture Mum's expression as I blurted out "rabbits" when she woke me in the morning. I'd look a right April fool before the day started!

PERHAPS it was because spring was on the way and the sun had been glinting through the early morning frosts that I felt this sudden longing for a boyfriend — or maybe I expected too much in the first months of my new job.

When I left school I had

32

Illustration by Caldwell.

and kissed her wrinkled cheek "— I'd better be getting home. I'll call by again later in the week."

She nodded and patted my arm.

"Don't you worry, Lucy. The right man will come along when you least expect him.

"And in the meantime —" her eyes twinkled "– a few 'hares' and 'rabbits' won't do any harm!"

I smiled wryly as I walked home, but that night found me lying pensively in bed and muttering "hares" as I snuggled under the duvet. I felt a right idiot!

embarked on a training programme in the largest retail store in town and I loved it. I thoroughly enjoyed dealing with the customers — well, most of them!

I met so many people — some very good-looking lads, too — but not one of them saw me as anyone more than an assistant there to help them. And time was marching on!

Gran measured the jumper she was knitting.

"You're only seventeen, you know, Lucy. Plenty of time for courting yet."

I nodded and sighed.

"Anyway, Gran —" I stood up

THE next morning, I remembered Gran's words as I opened my eyes and, glancing furtively around my bedroom, I whispered "rabbits".

Blushing furiously, I dressed for work.

It was a busy day. There were the usual April fool jokes being bandied around the store and, laughing, I succumbed. That day I was working in the confectionery department. As Easter was fast approaching the shelves were full of Easter eggs and delicious boxes of gift-wrapped chocolates.

It was around eleven when I looked up from rearranging the counter and saw the type of guy that invaded my dreams at night. Eyes the colour of the darkest chocolate egg, and looks that would turn the head of any spring chicken!

My heart did a flip. He was staring right back at me.

"Can I help you?" I managed to croak.

"Rabbits," he said, grinning at me.

I stared at him nonplussed, and then enlightenment dawned. This was why Gran had looked so smug. She had arranged the whole encounter!

I smiled to myself. Where on earth had she found this gorgeous man?

"Did Gran send you?"

He looked startled.

"Gran?"

"Yes." I blushed furiously. "My grandmother. I thought she might have sent you to see me."

He was watching me, an odd expression on his face.

"Well, I've certainly been sent to see you." He indicated the large box at his side. "But I don't think it was on your gran's instructions!" He chuckled and I squirmed with embarrassment.

"I'm sorry." I was at a loss for words. I could see Jane at the next counter, listening avidly.

"So Gran didn't send you?"

"Is this some kind of security code?" He looked mystified and I could see he was laughing at me.

"Shall we just say the boss sent me?"

I MANAGED a weak smile and mentally kicked myself. I was making a right April fool of myself, as well as a hash of this perfect opportunity for getting to know a really attractive man!

I saw Mrs Jones, the chief buyer, heading in my direction, and cringed. I was completely flustered.

"Ah, David." She took the young man's arm. "Have you brought the merchandise with you?"

"Indeed I have! Would you like to see them?"

"Come into my office."

She moved away briskly and, as he turned to follow her, he winked at me and picked up his box, leaving me totally confused.

I took an early lunch and, when I returned, I asked Jane about him. She said he had gone. I didn't know whether to be pleased or sorry. He was quite the dishiest man I had seen since I started work.

I had decided over lunch that Gran hadn't had anything to do with his appearance. I felt very gloomy. So much for "hares" and "rabbits"!

The next morning I couldn't believe my eyes. There, standing at my counter, was David. And beside him were several large boxes. "What are you doing here?"

"I brought more rabbits, but I'll let you display them!"

I watched him suspiciously as he opened a box. Inside were the most beautiful foil-wrapped chocolate rabbits.

"Chocolate rabbits!"

David was smiling.

"Of course! What did you expect, real ones?"

I grinned sheepishly.

"I'm sorry," I muttered. "I was confused."

"By your gran," he finished solemnly.

"I'll tell you what . . ." He started unpacking the chocolate rabbits. "How about meeting me for a coffee at lunchtime? You can tell me all about your gran and her rabbits!"

I nodded quickly. I wasn't going to waste a second chance.

"The café round the corner, one o'clock?"

"Yes, please," I managed to whisper.

With a cheery wave, he left, and I set about arranging the rabbits, a smile on my face.

L ATER, as we sipped our coffee, David explained that he was a student, making deliveries for the local chocolate factory during his holidays.

"It's a good enough job, and I meet some interesting people!" He chuckled and I blushed furiously.

"Now —" He leaned over the table and covered my hand with his. "Tell me about your gran."

It was difficult to explain why I had succumbed to the old March tradition, and I didn't mention my quest for a boyfriend, but when I had finished my faltering description of the good-luck superstition, David was smiling.

"I'd like to meet her!"

"Perhaps you will, one day."

"In the meantime, I was wondering . . ." David hesitated as his melting brown eyes gazed into mine. "Would you like to come to the cinema with me tonight? There's a good film showing."

I nodded eagerly.

"I'd love to!"

I didn't care what the film was but I asked anyway.

"One that I'm sure your gran would thoroughly approve of." David's face was serious.

"Oh?"

"'Watership Down'," he said, with a grin. ■

JILL leaned back in her chair and sipped her coffee. She was tired after her day at the library and was looking forward to the long weekend ahead.

The four days would make a welcome break, even though Easter wasn't really quite the same now that the twins were grown up.

by Jacqueline Spry.

"Do you remember how we used to hide the chocolate eggs in the garden for the children when they were little?" Jill asked her husband with more than a hint of nostalgia in her voice.

Andy half raised an eyebrow and smiled quizzically.

"Of course I do."

He hesitated.

"I know it's not the same now that Jenny and Mark have left home, but we'll make it a special Sunday."

DO YOU REMEMBER

Illustration by Siviglia.

Jill thought to herself that Easter was rather like Christmas. It only seemed magical when you had small children and could watch the delight and excitement in their eyes.

S HE could still picture Mark and Jenny racing round the garden with their little baskets, shrieking and squealing as they found a brightly-coloured egg hidden under a flowerpot or lodged on the mossy bank down by the sycamore tree.

Later, there would be the rivalry of counting out the eggs, as they vied with each other to see who had collected the most.

But it didn't really matter who had won, as Jill always made the twins share out the eggs equally.

Andy began to stack the dishwasher. As Jill sat finishing her coffee at the kitchen table, she realised that these days she often seemed to be dreaming of the past.

Nobody could say that she had been guilty of clinging on to her children — Jenny was spending a year out in Australia and Mark had just become a teacher up in Manchester.

But Jill did miss the twins not being near her and Andy.

She knew that sentences beginning with "Do you remember the time when . . .?" had started to crop up rather more frequently in her conversations with Andy. She half wondered if her husband was even a little annoyed about this.

Although Andy loved his children dearly and would spend hours chatting on the phone with Mark or Jenny, he didn't often mention the times when the twins were little. Surely he hadn't forgotten the old times?

Jill told herself not to be silly. As a mother, she'd been the one to have the children most of the time. She had stayed at home whilst Andy had done all those long shifts. He'd always worked hard and Jill knew that it was through his efforts that they had been able to buy such a lovely house and garden.

But now, Andy seemed to have had no trouble in moving on to the next stage in their lives. Jill knew that she should try to do the same. But somehow, it wasn't that easy.

"Will you be playing golf on Sunday?" she asked her husband.

"Yes, but only in the morning. We'll have the rest of the day for ourselves," he reassured her.

Jill didn't begrudge Andy his time spent on the golf course. It had been part of his routine to spend most Sunday mornings playing golf with his friend, Matthew.

Jill's mother had lived nearby and would come round every Sunday to entertain the twins whilst Jill was cooking lunch.

Jenny and Mark had been really close to Grandma Jean. She had known instinctively what interested them, sewing glamorous dresses for Jenny's dolls and even indulging Mark in the odd game of football, when none of his friends were around.

But Grandma Jean had died three years ago, just after the twins had left home to start their new lives at university.

"Would you like any more coffee?" Andy was asking.

"No, thanks."

She watched as he deftly emptied the powder into the small compartment and turned the dial until the dishwasher began to hum merrily.

He straightened up and looked at Jill. His brown eyes held hers for a few moments.

She felt he sensed what she'd been thinking, but he didn't mention Easter Sunday again.

Instead, he smiled.

"Come on! Let's go and watch those big cats."

A love of wildlife programmes was something that Jill and Andy had always shared.

JILL turned over lazily in bed. Through half closed eyes she saw bright sunshine beginning to stream through the crack between the curtains.

She felt Andy moving, then quietly he got out of bed. He must think she was still asleep, she told herself drowsily.

Without moving, Jill glanced at the clock. It was only seven o'clock. What on earth was he doing, getting up so early on a Sunday? He wouldn't be starting his game of golf for another couple of hours. Jill closed her eyes and drifted off to sleep again.

She was woken later by Andy coming into the bedroom with her cup of tea. He set it down on the bedside table.

"Happy Easter, darling!" He put his arms around his wife and held her close. Jill felt his warm lips on hers and snuggled up to him.

"I dreamed you'd already gone out to play golf," she murmured. Out of the corner of her eye she noticed it was nearly nine o'clock.

"Why did you get up so early?"

"Oh, I had a few things to do before I pick up Matthew," Andy replied rather vaguely.

He released his wife gently and went to draw back the curtains. The sunlight flooded into the room.

"Just perfect for an Easter morning! Take it easy, Jill. I'll be back well before lunch."

Andy kissed his wife goodbye and Jill sat up to drink her tea. She heard the front door close and, minutes later, the sound of Andy's car reversing down the drive and pulling away up the avenue. The house felt strangely empty.

Jill determinedly banished all thoughts of Easters gone by.

Those windows could do with a jolly good clean, she thought, noticing the sunlight showing up smears on the glass. It would keep her busy until it was time to start making the lunch.

Jill pulled on an old pair of jeans and a faded T-shirt and went downstairs. On the kitchen table she noticed a small wicker basket. Inside sparkled a silver-wrapped egg.

She was instantly touched by Andy's thoughtfulness. She ate her toast and then decided to have a nibble at the chocolate egg. As she took it out of the basket she noticed the folded piece of paper lying underneath.

Happy Easter, dearest Jill, and here's the first egg for your collection. To find the others just follow the five clues. Number one is easy, I hope!

Jill read the little verse that followed.

Down the path to the grassy nook,
Where Jenny used to read her book.

Jill ran her hands through her hair and thought hard. Yes! She knew what this meant.

Her eyes lit up with a childlike excitement as she put on her trainers and took the little basket out into the garden.

She almost skipped along the crazy paving and across the lawn to the point where it dipped down into a little hollow. She stopped dead in her tracks.

She thought she saw a little girl with a blonde bob in a gingham dress, sitting on an old blanket. She was engrossed in a storybook; her favourite tale of "The Magic Faraway Tree".

Jill caught her breath. She saw her young daughter turn towards her, smiling and saying, "This bit's brilliant, Mummy!"

Jill stood still and a lump came to her throat. Slowly, the vision faded and she walked slowly forward. She found the egg wrapped in blue, nestling in the long tufts of grass. She picked it up and saw the next clue.

By a window, high not low,
A maddening red might start to glow.

If the first clue had been simple, this one was certainly difficult. Jill knew Andy's love of cryptic crosswords and smiled to herself.

She made her way back to the house and started to look at the windows. Nothing red or glowing there. She walked round to the front of the house, stared up again, but found nothing.

Jill went inside and up the stairs. She peered at the windows in their bedroom, in the bathroom and in Jenny's room.

Finally, she went into Mark's old bedroom and gave a little gasp of surprise. On the table by the window she saw his favourite toy, a Dalek,

The Courtship

*T*HE years flew by and then one day,
  When Kate was seventeen,
It dawned on Joe she was the prettiest
Girl he'd ever seen.

And now he saw his little friend
In quite a different way;
No longer was she just the child
With whom he used to play.

When had that little pigtailed girl
Become this lady fair?
Gentle, elegant and sweet,
Her smile beyond compare?

He suddenly felt very shy
And wondered what she'd say
If he suggested that they might
Go walking out one day.

                – Alice Drury.

scratched and a little battered now.

Mark had never let his mother get rid of the Dalek. Andy must have unearthed it from the cupboard.

Oh, that toy had driven Jill mad as it had made its way across the kitchen floor with red flashing lights, screaming "Exterminate!" to anybody unlucky enough to get in its way.

Maddening, too, had been the number of batteries it consumed! And yet, Mark had loved this toy more than all his others.

Jill looked towards the bed and imagined a small boy with dark curls, lying asleep, clutching the red Dalek, She remembered how she used to smooth away the little frown from his face before she kissed him goodnight.

The picture in her head gradually dissolved and Jill turned back to the window. She collected a red egg from its place by the side of the Dalek and read the third clue.

A sticky one, dear Jill, I know
Once you've found Fluffs, not far to go.

Fluffs was their long-haired ginger cat. They'd got him as a kitten when Mark and Jenny were young, and Fluffs had turned out to be just as playful and mischievous as the twins. But now he was nearly sixteen and had settled down to a staid old age.

Jill searched the garden, to no avail. Fluffs was probably having his morning nap. She went into the conservatory. There he was, sleeping peacefully on a nest made out of Andy's old pullovers.

He yawned and half opened one eye. Jill felt under the worn wool and Fluffs got up slowly, arching his back, unhappy at being disturbed. Jill pulled out a softened chocolate egg. She realised now what Andy had meant by sticky. This egg had started to melt — it was one she definitely wouldn't be eating!

JILL just had time to retrieve the fourth clue before Fluffs settled back into his rightful place.

Just be bold and follow your nose
To Grandma Jean's favourite rose.

Outside again in the warm sunshine, Jill surveyed the rose bed. Grandma Jean had been an expert on roses and had passed her knowledge on to her daughter.

Jill knew exactly which rose was "Peace", even though no buds, let alone flowers, were showing yet.

She moved closer and felt her mother's presence. She could almost see Grandma Jean bending down, and hear her lilting voice:

"Now you need to prune just above this little bud here."

Jill watched the knife glint in her mother's worn hands as it sliced through the stem, leaving the energy to sap into a new, strong shoot which would eventually be crowned with golden blooms.

Jill's mother had always been wise. She had been the one who knew that Andy was the right man for her daughter, when Jill brought him home the first time to meet her parents.

Jill missed her mother's good advice and reassurance and hoped that she, too, would be able to offer these qualities to Mark and Jenny in their adult lives.

A golden egg lay at the base of the rose and Jill picked it up, along with the final clue. Except it wasn't really a clue — it was more like an instruction.

Please don't cook lunch, my darling Jill,
We're going out to Ivy Mill.

How romantic! It was at Ivy Mill down by the river that Andy had proposed to Jill twenty-seven years ago. He'd borrowed his father's old Ford especially to take her out, and Jill knew he must have had to save up for weeks to pay for their special meal. She'd been so happy that night as they'd planned their future together.

SUDDENLY, it dawned on Jill how lucky they had been. The future they had planned had now become their happy past. She knew she was ready to move on. There was a whole host of experiences waiting for her and Andy — experiences that would create the next set of wonderful memories.

Dear, kind, thoughtful Andy! He had got up early especially to plan this lovely surprise for her. How could she have doubted that he, too, held memories like treasures in his heart? Maybe he didn't talk about them so often but that didn't mean that he had forgotten.

She ran her fingers gently over the eggs in the wicker basket. Each one represented one of her loved ones.

Jill went upstairs. Window cleaning could wait for another day! She changed into the yellow outfit she had bought especially for Easter. She was just fastening the pair of earrings that Andy had bought for her on their engagement when she heard his car draw up in the drive.

Jill went to the window and opened it wide.

"I've filled the basket. Thank you for a wonderful trip down memory lane!"

Andy beamed broadly and gazed up at his wife. He thought she looked as radiant as she had done twenty-seven years ago.

"And now I'm ready!" Jill smiled eagerly.

Andy heard the conviction in her voice and understood just what she meant. ∎

PRIMROSE AMBER put the letter down on the table, and couldn't help noticing, as she did so, that her hands were shaking.

It was amazing that it had reached her, really. She'd been away from the old house for over two years now. The new people must have been kind enough to send it on.

She didn't need to open it to know who it was from. The writing on the envelope gave that away.

After all these years — she could hardly believe it. She gave herself a little shake to prove she wasn't dreaming.

But when she looked again it was still there.

It was from Buffalo Bill. At least, that was what her mother had called him.

"But his name isn't Bill," Primrose had protested. "It's Lawrence. Why do you call him that?"

Her mother had made a noise that would have been called a snort had it come from someone she disapproved of. And her mother definitely disapproved of Lawrence.

"He's a cowboy — by nature if not by calling. He may spin yarns instead of ropes, but it comes to the same thing in the end."

"He doesn't . . ." Primrose had

Illustration by Gerard Fay.

tried to defend him, but her mother wasn't having it.

"Oh, doesn't he? What about the time he told us he rescued a child from a fierce dog? It turned out to be that miniature poodle of Mrs Worley's!

"And what about the prize he said he got for travel writing? The Kiddies' Korner in the local paper had sent him a pound for his piece on 'My Best Holiday'!"

"You're not being fair. He doesn't tell lies," Primrose had protested weakly.

"He romances." Her mother had pronounced the word as if romancing was a very nasty habit. "He's not trustworthy. You mark my words, Primrose. You're wasting your time with him.

"He'll never settle down. Here today, gone tomorrow. I know you won't take any notice of me — young people never take advice

months, postcards had come regularly, bearing exotic stamps and views of faraway cities. Then they became less frequent, until finally they stopped all together.

Primrose, unable to write to a man who had no address, waited for news. Weeks lengthened into months, and then into years.

"Heard from Buffalo Bill

Yesterday Once More

by M.E. Bickerstaffe.

from their elders. But you'll see, mark my words!"

Primrose had simply tossed her head. But her mother had been right. It wasn't long before Lawrence had decided that he wanted to see the world.

COME with me, Primmie. We'll see everything there is to see — the Golden Gate Bridge, the Taj Mahal, the Great Barrier Reef."

"I can't," she had protested. "I can't just go off, maybe for years, and leave my mother by herself. It wouldn't be right."

And so, in the end, Lawrence had gone on his own. For a few

lately?" her mother would ask sometimes. "No? Well, I did warn you."

* * * *

Time went by. Although she told herself firmly that she had put Lawrence behind her, Primrose never met another man who measured up to him.

After her mother died she sold the big family house and moved into a bungalow, a more suitable dwelling for a single lady of a certain age.

Occasionally she remembered Lawrence and wondered where he was. Had he settled in some far-flung spot?

And now, suddenly, here he was — or at least his letter was. Primrose read it through yet again.

I was always sorry that we drifted apart the way we did. I finally settled down and got married, although the marriage didn't last long. But I never forgot you, Primmie, and I would love to see you again.

It so happens that I have business in Melchester on the 25th of this month. Would it be too much to ask you to meet me in the old place, under the clock at the railway station? I shall wait there anyway, from 12 until 12.30. If you don't turn up I shall understand. If you do — well, I'm sure we'll have a lot to talk about.

Typically, he still hadn't included an address or telephone number, so if she wanted to contact him she would have to turn up at the meeting place.

Cheek, Primrose thought, in a sudden burst of anger. He seems to think I've been waiting for him all these years! I've a good mind not to go.

But in her heart she knew she would be there. It's just curiosity, she told herself. I'm just interested to see what he's like now, hear how his life's been.

Her mother's photograph regarded her sceptically from the mantelpiece. Primrose picked up the frame and repositioned it on the far corner of the bookcase.

O N the 25th she put on her best coat, and the shoes with the little heels. She had had her hair done the previous day, but now it seemed too smooth, too neat.

She applied some lipstick, which she hardly ever wore, and then scrubbed it off again. It's no good trying to look anything but what I am, she thought.

I'm thirty years older. The last time he saw me, I was fair. Now I'm grey. I've put on some weight. He probably won't even recognise me.

She arrived at the station early and aimlessly wandered through the shops on the concourse, glancing at her watch every few minutes.

I'll wait until 12.15, she decided. I don't want to seem too eager. Then, suddenly, it was 12.20. I shall be late, she thought in a panic.

From the doorway of the shop she was in she could see the clock — the same big round clock under which she had waited for Lawrence so many times in days gone by. And there, glimpsed between the hurrying figures of people going to and from the platforms, he was.

He looked exactly the same as when she had seen him last — the set of the shoulders, the dark curly hair, the straight nose. She could see his profile clearly, as he chatted to an elderly man who leaned on a stick.

Primrose hesitated. The courage she had summoned up for this meeting had vanished. I'm an old woman, she thought, and he hasn't aged at all. I can't, I simply can't face him.

She hurried to the escalator that led down to the street. It had been a mistake to come, but at least she had got away before it was too late.

She was halfway down the moving stairs when the thought suddenly struck her. Wait a minute — if I'm thirty years older, so is he. He can't be that upright, dark-haired young man!

She hurried to the bottom of the escalator and immediately began to run back up the one that led to the station.

As she reached the concourse again, the hands of the clock pointed to half-past twelve. Would he still be waiting?

The young man had gone, but the older one was still there. Even as she saw this, she realised that he was preparing to leave.

"Stop!" Primrose shouted.

HE looked round, startled, and she could see that he was Lawrence. The white hair, the stooped shoulders, the walking stick — these were not important. It was her Lawrence.

"Primmie! I'd decided you weren't coming."

"I'm sorry," she said, slightly out of breath. "But I'm here now."

"So you are." His smile was just as she remembered it. "You know, I almost didn't come myself — cold feet. But my son persuaded me. He said it wasn't fair.

"He actually came with me, to make sure that I didn't lose my nerve. He's only just gone."

So that's who the young man was, Primrose thought. She was about to say that he was very like his dad and then remembered that she was supposed to have just arrived.

"I'm sorry to have missed him," she said instead.

Lawrence didn't answer her directly. He was looking at her in just the same way as he used to, all those years ago.

"You haven't changed a bit," he said. "It's amazing."

She blushed at the compliment.

"And you . . ."

"Oh," he interrupted, shaking his head. "I haven't worn as well as you. I smashed my leg up — can't do without this walking stick now."

"What happened?" Primrose asked.

Recalling the tall stories, she wondered what sort of colourful yarn he would have to tell.

A mountaineering mishap? A gun-shot wound?

Lawrence caught her eye and grinned, and she knew that he was thinking the same thing.

"As a matter of fact," he said, "I tripped over a paving-stone."

Primrose began to laugh as they moved off together. It seemed that Buffalo Bill had grown up at last. ∎

One Summer Long Ago

by Pamela Kavanagh.

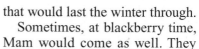

BLACKBERRY time again, Joy thought, sinking down on the garden seat in the sun. Her mind went back to another September, when she was eighteen, and the days stretched enticingly ahead.

Westhope had been more of a hamlet then, and Moss Cottage had stood on the edge, not crowded in with houses as it was now. Her father had grown roses in the front garden and cabbages and potatoes in the back.

"You could put an apple tree by the gate, Fred," Mam once said. "A Bramley, or a Cox's Pippin."

"What, instead of my Damasks?" Father said. "Never!"

"You can't eat roses. A nice apple pie now, or a crumble . . ."

Mam was like that. Stomachs came first — understandable, with five hungry mouths to feed. Baking, bottling, jamming — never a berry wasted. Being the only girl in the family, it fell to Joy to gather the fruit for the jam that would last the winter through.

Sometimes, at blackberry time, Mam would come as well. They would make an event of it, taking a picnic and eating it under a shady tree whilst batting off the pestering wasps and midges.

Nipping little insects never bothered Mam, but Joy suffered cruelly, coming up in fiery bumps which itched to distraction.

ON this remembered occasion, Joy had gone alone. She had been prepared, drenched in oil of citronella to ward off the flies, and carrying baskets, food and lemonade, and a walking stick to bring down the juiciest berries, which always seemed to grow out of reach.

Dressed in her old blue gingham — it never did to doll up, clothing always got snagged on the briars — with a battered panama on her curls, she

48

Illustration by M.Thorsen.

er,

49

felt ready for anything.

Anything except meeting another gatherer, and a personable one at that . . .

The best berries grew in a sheltered valley with a narrow lane winding steeply down to the brook. Methodically, Joy started at the top, picking deftly, her thoughts drifting, lulled by the warmth, the scent of grass and flowers and the distant music of water trickling over brown rocks.

"Curses!" A voice broke into her reverie.

Joy started, then peered curiously through a gap in the brambles. A young fellow, tallish, with wild brown hair and a thin face, was trying with some difficulty to bind a torn finger with his handkerchief.

"Shall I do that for you?" Joy asked.

The man gazed about him in puzzlement.

"I'm here," Joy said. "On the other side."

"Ah! One moment. I'll be right with you."

THERE was a rustling in the bushes and he appeared, sporting a few more scratches for his trouble. Hazel eyes flicked over her with amusement, and Joy wished she had worn her pink cotton at the very least. Uncomfortably conscious of the pungent whiff of citrus about her person, she inspected the wound.

"First, it needs cleaning up. Let's go down to the brook."

"All right," he said affably. He spoke with what Joy's mother would have termed an educated voice, and as they went down to the water Joy answered him in her slow, sweet village tones.

Injury sorted, she folded the handkerchief and neatly bandaged the hand.

"Florence Nightingale, my thanks."

"My name's Joy," she said. "Joy Rogers."

"And I'm Peter Grant. Pleased to meet you, Joy."

He offered his bound hand, grinned ruefully and let it fall again to his side.

"Too bad there isn't a pub close by. I'm parched."

"I've got some lemonade. You're welcome to some. Lunch, too. It's only Mam's wholemeal loaf and some cheddar, but there's plenty."

He grinned.

"Thank you, that sounds splendid."

They sat on the bank, sharing the food and chatting for all the world as if they had known each other always. Peter was a medical student, visiting the north-west on a walking holiday.

"I would have thought," Joy said with mock severity, "that someone learning to be a doctor would have known about treating scratches."

"Ah, but they've never shown us how to cope one-handed, you see," he answered solemnly. They both laughed.

"My holiday has just flown. Only another ten days and then I'm due back in Edinburgh."

"Scotland," Joy said with envy.

She confided how she badly wanted to train as a secretary and couldn't because the college was too far away to travel to each day.

"You could always take lodgings and come home at weekends," Peter suggested.

"Couldn't. Mam needs help in the house. All that washing and cooking." Joy sighed. "I would so love a career. It's all right for our Robbie and Mark. I wish I'd been born a boy, then it wouldn't be a problem."

Peter's eyes twinkled.

"I'm rather glad you weren't. I like you as you are!"

She coloured up and he smiled warmly at her.

"Now, about these blackberries. Want me to help pick?"

They spent the afternoon gathering, and Joy went home with her two baskets brimming with fruit. She didn't mention Peter. Mam would only fuss, and besides, though they had parted on the understanding that they would meet again the next day, Joy decided to reserve judgement.

You never knew with boys. In her experience, if something more interesting came along, they were quite likely to stand you up.

BUT Peter was there, and Joy was thankful she had made an effort with her appearance. She wore a pretty summer frock in a fresh cotton print, straw hat with trailing pink ribbons, and sandals on her feet. There was no citronella this time, but a dab of rosewater which she prayed would not draw the midges.

If Mam wondered about the outfit she made no comment, and Peter's eyes lit up when he saw her, stepping lightly towards him along the lane, a basket in each hand.

"More blackberries? Your mother must be making jam for the troops!"

"Believe me," Joy said, "it takes pounds and pounds of fruit to make bramble jelly. Yesterday's went into pies."

Peter licked his lips.

"Blackberry apple pie with hot custard! Yum!"

Tempted to ask him back with her for supper, Joy thought again. There'd only be ructions afterwards. Mam liked at least a week's notice if company was expected.

"Where shall we pick today?" she said instead. "The spinney's good for fruit. Let's try there."

Again they managed to fill the baskets, and then they had their picnic lunch under the trees. Peter had brought food today; chicken, salad and fruit. There was a bottle of wine, too, but Joy shook her head.

"I daren't. Mam would scalp me if she smelled a hint on me."

"I think," Peter said slowly, "that a certain young woman needs to stand up for herself a bit. If my sister Avril wanted a glass of plonk, she'd have one."

"Your Avril doesn't live in Westhope. If she took a drink here she'd be branded for life as being no better than she should be!"

She chuckled to lighten the words, yet much later, tucked up in her warm bed, Joy pondered seriously on her life in the small country village. In her heart she knew she wanted to get away, but how could she leave Mam and Father and the boys, and everything else that was dear to her?

Moss Cottage was home, and always would be. Of course she could never leave.

And on that positive note she fell asleep. But the first tiny seeds of discontent had been inexorably sown.

T HE weather held and she and Peter met each day, always discreetly, always finding more berries on the bushes to give credence to Joy's absence from home. Pots of bramble jelly were made and stored away in ruby ranks on the pantry shelf.

On the day before Peter was due to travel back north, they were both quiet.

"I'll miss you," he said suddenly. "Will you write? I promise I'll reply."

Joy hesitated.

"Mam will wonder if I get letters with a Scottish postmark."

"Oh, for goodness' sake!" Peter exploded. "We're in the 1920s now! All that Victorian stuff went out with the last century."

"Not in Westhope it didn't."

"Then get yourself out of here. Show them you've got a life to live. Grow up!"

"I thought I was being grown up," Joy snapped, bristling. "What about responsibility? They're my parents. I can't just walk out on them."

North Berwick

N ORTH BERWICK lies close to the mouth of the Firth, just half an hour's drive from Edinburgh.

Attracted by a healthy climate, fine sands, the seaside and pleasant surroundings, visitors began to flock here in their thousands in Victorian times.

Golfers, though, never needed another excuse to play the famous links and those at nearby Muirfield. In fact, golf was played here as early as the 17th century!

53

"No-one's asking you to!"

"You are."

They fought on. It was a stupid quarrel, bitter and rancorous. It ended with Joy close to tears and Peter tight-faced and silent. Gathering up the abandoned picnic things, they parted company. Joy headed straight for home.

Running upstairs, she flung herself on her bed and wept. Their lovely, lovely interlude was ruined. It wasn't fair!

The sound of someone knocking on the door, and then voices when her mother went to answer the summons, barely registered. Then Mam called.

"Joy, love! Someone asking for you."

She got up, splashed her hot cheeks with cooling water and tidied her hair. Then she went downstairs.

Peter was in the kitchen, totally at home, a steaming cup of tea and a slice of pie in a dish before him.

"Hello," he greeted her. "You forgot something."

He pointed to the fruit baskets which Joy in her haste had left under the hedge.

Mam watched, her sharp blue gaze darting from one cautious young face to the other.

"Not more blackberries," she said, lips twitching. "Mercy me, our Joy. After this week I don't think I ever want to see another one again!"

BEAMING, Joy looked up to see her husband coming into the garden. Peter's dark hair was white now and his thin face was lined, but his grin was just as youthful and his hazel eyes were warm with love as he approached her.

"There you are. Fancy a trip out?"

"Lovely," Joy said, rising. "Surgery over, is it?"

"I've managed to wangle the afternoon off. It's such a beautiful day I thought we might go for a spin down memory lane."

They exchanged a telling glance.

"I'll never forget your face when you saw me sitting in the kitchen and your mother stuffing me with food. I'd dreaded meeting her — I thought she must have been a harridan! But she wasn't at all."

"Only because she fell for your charms."

"Oh, well." He affected a shrug. "How could she help it?"

"So modest!" Joy tutted. "Still, it gave me the shove I needed. I got that typist's certificate — and the best husband in the world as well."

"Bless you. Are you coming? We've a family invasion tonight, remember. You can make us a pie. No prizes for guessing what sort."

"It's got to be blackberry," she said, taking his arm with a smile. "I'll even help you pick." ■

by Linda
Chloe Elmon.

Illustration by Bernard Dowling.

HER DREAM HOME

A S Jenny prepared the fish for Martin's
dinner, her glance strayed through the wide
kitchen window. She smiled with satisfaction
at her handiwork.

It had taken her all day to dig up the old buddleia and
reorganise the space into a new flower-bed but, in a few

months, the bedraggled new plants would surge into life and look a picture.

As Jenny stirred the sauce, her gaze lingered on the blend of shapes and colours she'd achieved over the years in the garden. Or at least in the bit she could see, because beyond the wide lawn a row of dwarf cypresses and Japanese acers shielded the extensive lower part from her scrutiny.

She'd planted the acers when Mark was doing his GCSEs, and the cypresses went in around the time young Andrew had discovered that the girl in the garden centre wasn't quite as soppy as he'd thought the year before when he was thirteen and football mad. In a way, the trees and shrubs were like living pages from a family diary, timing events and memories.

THE sound of Martin's car in the drive brought Jenny back to reality. "First the bad news," Martin said, once he'd kissed her and changed out of his business suit. He leaned over her shoulder to sample the sauce.

"I've been summoned to head office for the rest of the week. I'll be away sharp tomorrow morning."

"Oh, Martin," Jenny said. Time at home was precious, and an unexpected trip away was a blow to both of them.

"Still, it can't be helped. Hey! That sauce isn't bad," he said.

Jenny quickly slipped the lid back on the pot before he could get at it again.

"It's for eating with the fish, not for you to slurp beforehand. Now, what's the good news? I presume there is some." She turned back to the sink.

"Good enough for a bottle of sparkling wine, I should think," he said, opening the fridge door. "How do you fancy a move?"

Jenny's gaze was suddenly frozen on the trim lawn and flower-beds. She didn't turn round immediately. Martin's hand was on her shoulder and his other hand, clutching the bottle of wine, circled her waist.

"No, don't say anything. Just let the idea mull round in your mind while I'm away. Sort of test the water. Nothing's settled yet, but it looks certain that the trip to head office is to see how I'd feel about taking over from old Ted Harding."

The significance of this unfroze Jenny's gaze. She turned quickly.

"Oh, Martin! They're really going to offer you Ted's job? That's marvellous. Not that you don't deserve it. Oh, put that bottle away. This is a champagne moment."

Much later, Jenny was still lying awake while Martin slept. They'd talked about what the new job would mean for their social life — the new challenges and commitments, the public functions.

Jenny laughingly sketched out demands for an entire new wardrobe. Ted Harding's statuesque wife would be a hard act to follow as the company's first lady, but Jenny relished the thought.

They contemplated what the sharp increase in Martin's salary and benefits would mean for Mark and Andrew, where they might go for exotic holidays, how delighted for them their relatives and friends would be.

Martin was brimming over with plans for improvements in the business and how he might profitably move the company forward.

But it wasn't the exciting prospects but the thought of moving from her lovely, familiar home which kept Jenny awake while Martin snored gently. It was a lot to think about.

I'LL be back on Friday," Martin said the next morning, over a hurried breakfast. "By then it should be official. We'll call Mum and Dad when they get back on Friday night and tell them. The kids as well. You can be thinking about the posh house you always said you wanted."

In the early days, before the boys were born, they had often passed a cheap evening on the couch thumbing through a glossy magazine of glorious houses, expensive cars and gorgeously attired couples — daydreaming of the future.

On long walks in the country, they paused to gaze at substantial detached houses in manicured grounds, pretending the place was theirs.

"Those two windows in the middle we'll make the master bedroom. They've got the best view. The kids can have the end rooms," Martin would say, pointing at the house.

"And those curtains have to go. They're too gaudy," Jenny would chip in.

"And we'll have glossy blue doors and windows. They'll look better with the pale stone. And there's plenty of room for your hothouse."

Jenny had always wanted a vast glasshouse conservatory where she could grow huge exotic indoor plants, and a large fully equipped Spanish-style kitchen with a range and dangling copper pots.

Martin had dreamed of a panelled, book-lined study and a large garage with enough room for a workshop bench. They'd both had visions of a sweeping gravel drive leading to an ornate entrance with lawns and flower-beds.

The master bedroom would contain a large four-poster bed with floaty drapes. Such was their dream house.

They'd bought their first small, terraced home a few months before Mark had been born. As time passed, they'd moved to better areas.

But during the last fifteen years, although Martin had been promoted several times, they'd remained where they were, not wishing to disrupt the children's schooling.

The comfortable detached house with its quiet neighbourhood, another plus for the children, had suited them.

Now, the boys had left home and, with this big promotion, there was nothing to prevent Martin and Jenny climbing further up the housing ladder towards their ideal.

JENNY went out into the garden with its shade and feeling of peace and calm. When they'd first bought the house, it had been a complete wilderness.

She'd designed the whole garden from scratch. Martin had done the heavy work, using it as a therapy against the pressures of the office and as a way of easing any stress. He'd loved the results as much as Jenny.

Spectrum Colour Library.

ROTHE

They'd played cricket and football with the boys on the lawn during the summers and had barbecues and outdoor dinners galore. The thought of leaving it, and the memories, was heartbreaking.

But that wasn't all. The feeling of what it would mean to leave the familiar district struck her when she walked into the town's lovely, tree-lined square.

It was sedate, ordered and very pretty. Behind the town was the beginning of the moors and the wide-open spaces she loved dearly.

As if to aggravate the wound, she met several of her favourite people in the first ten minutes of her shopping trip, and they seemed genuinely delighted to see her. The more she thought about it, the more she realised just how many friends they'd made in the town.

"Kept back a pair of lovely steaks specially for you, Mrs Lassiter.

AY Isle Of Bute

Now known as a holiday resort, thanks historically to the huge rise in the industrial population of Glasgow, Rothesay has many amenities for sport and entertainment. Add that to winter gardens, an indoor swimming pool, facilities for rowing excursions and sea angling and you can see why the Glasgow crowd on holiday really enjoyed going "doon the watter"!

The town, with its bright and unusual architecture, hugs the coast and looks directly across the Kyles of Bute to Argyll. The annual Clyde Yachting Fortnight is held in what are, for its purposes, the admirable circumstances of Rothesay Bay.

Rothesay also has a castle, built around 1098, which is one of the most remarkable mediaeval castles in Scotland. Its plan is unique, and the ruin is definitely worth a visit.

Scotch Beef," Mr Hall, the butcher, said.

Vera in the newsagent's wanted to talk about the plans for the amateur dramatic society's next production. Jenny had shared stage manager's duties and enjoyed it hugely.

"It'll be our first musical. It'll be fantastic, Jenny," Vera enthused as Jenny paid for the papers.

When she got back to the house she sat on the bench by the little ornamental pond with its sundial island which Martin had built. And she thought about what a move would mean to him.

His mum and dad were getting on and, at the moment, he was only able to see them a few times a year. A move to London would also mean proximity to loads of theatres, restaurants, exhibitions and galleries, all of which Martin enjoyed immensely. As a student he'd had a bedsit near Earl's Court.

"I don't recall working much," he'd said. "We always seemed to be out at museums, reviews, concerts or parties."

Jenny had found a niche for herself in this market town, but now Martin deserved to enjoy the fruits of his labours which the new job could offer. He'd always claimed that the capital city was dynamic and full of energy. He could mix with other business high-flyers and benefit from the interaction.

Surely it was his due now that he'd made sure his sons had the best possible start in life and had worked so hard to provide a secure home and future for Jenny?

ON Friday afternoon, Martin called.

"I've got the job! I take over in a couple of months."

He sounded quietly calm but Jenny could tell he was holding in his excitement.

"I'll be home later tonight and we'll call the kids and Mum and Dad."

After she'd put the phone down she reflected that it was appropriate that their occupation of the house should end on a high point. There had been plenty of proud and thrilling moments for the family over the years.

The sun broke through the scattered clouds as Jenny went out on to the lawn and looked round at the beautiful things she'd created. It would be tough to give it up but there was no earthly reason why she couldn't do it again. She was pretty tough herself.

And in London there would be even more opportunities for her to develop a packed and fulfilling life. If they chose the area carefully, the traffic, crime, pollution, noise and frantic bustle Jenny had always associated with the city need not be so invasive. She would make lots of new friends. She was strong-willed. She was determined that Martin would get his chance.

She toured the large garden, memories triggered by the sight of the various plants and features.

Mark skinning his knee on his first attempt to climb the cherry tree . . . toddler Andrew paddling in the pond on a hot day, trying to catch the goldfish with his hands . . . Martin stripped to the waist and glistening with sweat as he hacked through the undergrowth which eventually became the vegetable patch . . . the whole family having an "at home picnic" in the little glade Jenny had created behind the rhododendrons.

Everywhere she looked held a memory, and she had tears in her eyes when she went back into the house.

The tears would have to be banished later. Martin must not know how she felt, or for her sake alone he would sacrifice a move to the city and forgo his own wishes to return to the home of his parents. She couldn't be so selfish. He'd worked hard to achieve his long-cherished visions of a dream house.

ON his return Martin basked in congratulations now the news was official. His parents and the children showed their delight in their characteristic ways.

Later, he and Jenny sat together on the sofa and sipped glasses of wine.

"Well, my love, together we did it." He pulled her closer and kissed the top of her head.

"It doesn't seem so long ago when we started out," she said, snuggling into him.

"No. The years have flown. Maybe they've seemed so fast because they were so good." There was a pause for thought. "Oh! I've got something for you. I've kept this in the bottom drawer of every office desk I've had since the beginning."

He reached into his briefcase and pulled out a large, creased envelope.

"I've been keeping it for today."

Intrigued, she peeked inside. The envelope contained a twenty-five-year-old copy of "House & Garden". She recalled it instantly and her eyes were bright with tears at the memory.

It was the copy which had featured their idea of the perfect dream house. Their youthful aim. She remembered their delight at coming across the pictures of the lovely house which matched all their wishes. Slowly, Jenny leafed through the magazine, looking at the past.

Little did Martin realise that such a house was no longer her dream.

Without her meaning it, Jenny's face must have revealed her innermost thoughts, because Martin's next words surprised her.

"Jen, we've come this far together because we've always told each other what was on our minds. We've never had any secrets. We were always honest with each other."

Jenny looked at the magazine. He'd kept it for all that time. It was his dream, and one he was obviously convinced she still shared.

And in a way, she supposed she still did. She loved him as much as ever, would go with him wherever his dream took him.

"Martin, you know something? I'll live absolutely anywhere that makes you happy, but I'm not bothered about getting the classiest, swishest, illustrated magazine house any more. My dream house is where my family calls home. Right here and now, with you. This is my dream house."

Jenny held her breath, but his reaction took her by surprise.

"Oh, I knew I married the right woman!" Martin said with conviction, and hugged her fiercely.

"I was wondering how to tell you the same thing. If you'd still felt you needed your dream house I'd have gone wherever you wanted, but here's where most of our dreams came true.

"You can't just buy a real home, or pick it out of a magazine. A home's something you have to make yourself."

The old magazine slipped to the floor as she turned in his arms, but neither of them gave it another thought. ■

The Engagement

*K*ATE and Joe were happy
In their precious courtship days
Getting well acquainted with
Each other's little ways.

And very soon they realised
How close they had become,
And in their hearts they had a wish
That they should be as one.

When Joe proposed that they should wed
Kate blushed and whispered, "yes".
Her parents both approved the match
And wished them happiness.

They planned to wait a little while
Before they settled down
While Joe trained as a banker
In a busy, far-off town.

It broke their hearts to be apart,
But while Joe was away
Kate made the preparations
For their coming wedding day.

– Alice Drury.

The One That Got Away

by Katharine Swartz.

Illustration by David Young.

U NCLE FELIX! What a lovely surprise." Felix smiled affectionately at his niece as he climbed out of his car. Every once in a while he liked to stop by her family's cottage. He would give them a quick telephone call to check if they were home, and then he'd hop in his car.

That was the great thing about Lisa and her family. They never minded his unexpected visits; they just smiled and asked how long he planned to stay.

"Just a couple of days," Felix promised with a wink. "Is there a bed for me?"

"There's always a bed for you here, Uncle Felix," Lisa replied.

Felix grinned. He had started coming to Lisa's cottage in the country after his wife, Ruth, had died. He had been lonely and restless then.

Lisa, her husband, Dan, and their son, Warren, then just a chubby toddler, had made him feel really welcome. He had kept coming after that, almost out of habit, but mostly because he enjoyed the visits. And, of course, there was great fishing in the nearby river.

E VER since he had been a small boy, Felix had loved fishing. His friends always teased him about his grand fishing stories.

"It's always the one that gets away, isn't it, Felix?" they would say, with knowing nods and winks.

Felix freely admitted he exaggerated about the size of the fish he caught, and more importantly, the ones he didn't catch. That was half the fun of fishing — the art of exaggeration.

When he had started coming to Lisa's cottage, he had hoped to pass on his love of fishing to young Warren. And every time he visited, Warren duly accompanied Felix out in the rowing boat, where they would sit with their lines dangling in the water, waiting for the big one.

"There's one in every stretch of water," Felix told Warren complacently. "The big fish that you just never manage to catch. There's definitely one in this lake."

"How do you know?" Warren asked, his face filled with boyish curiosity.

Felix tapped his temple knowingly.

"Instinct. This one's a real old lady."

Felix let Warren pick a name for the fish because every big uncaught catch needed a name.

"Molly," Warren decided, because that was the name of a girl at school who teased him about his freckles.

"Molly it is." Felix shouted towards the depths of the lake. "We know you're out there, Molly! It's just a matter of time!"

He leaned back, chuckling.

"Enough fishing for today. I've scared them all away now."

* * * *

Now, Felix stood outside the cottage, breathing in the fresh scent of the pine trees, enjoying the sight of the wind rippling across the surface of the lake.

The sound of the door opening and closing behind him startled Felix out of his reverie.

"I'm going fishing. Are you coming with me, Warren?" he asked automatically.

"Nah, it's not worth it." Warren, now fourteen and sprouting some stubble on his chin, shook his head. "I never catch anything."

"What?" Felix drew himself up, indignant. "What do you mean, you never catch anything? You caught four or five last summer!"

"Three," Warren corrected him. "And they were tiny. You threw them back in, Uncle Felix. Don't you remember?"

"Did I?" Felix sighed. Actually, he often threw fish back in, unless it was one that could be eaten.

He was an old softie, he knew that.

"Molly's still out there, Warren," he told his nephew. "The grandmother of all rainbow trout. Don't you want to catch her?"

"Uncle Felix," Warren replied, with something close to martyrdom, "we've been fishing together since I was four and we've never even seen Molly. I don't think she's real."

"What?" Felix couldn't believe his ears. He knew he had the habit of telling some tall tales when it came to fishing, but he was sure that Molly was real. She had to be.

"Have more faith!" he scoffed, trying to laugh. "Come on, Warren. The wind is just right. If we're really quiet, we'll get more than a nibble."

Warren shook his head and headed back inside.

"Sorry, Uncle Felix. I'm going back on the internet."

"Internet?" Felix muttered. What was the world coming to? Boys who spent the summer in a cottage should be outside, running barefoot through the grass, taking flying dives into the cool, clear water, and fishing. They shouldn't be cooped up inside, fiddling with some stupid computer!

FELIX went out in the old rowing boat by himself, the oars creaking as he rowed himself into the middle of the lake, and sat there for over an hour, his fishing line dangling in the water.

Unfortunately, he didn't catch anything. He didn't even have a nibble. His mouth pressed into a thin line, he silently rowed back to the shore and got ready for supper.

"What is it with young Warren?" he asked Lisa as he helped her with the washing up after their meal. "He refused to go fishing with me today!"

"Did he?" Lisa avoided meeting his eye. "Well, I suppose he's interested in other things now, Uncle Felix."

Felix was too sharp not to realise Lisa was hiding something.

"But he's always loved fishing," he argued. "Even when we didn't catch anything!"

"I know, Uncle Felix." Lisa hid a smile."If you want to know the truth, I think the real problem is that Warren is fourteen, not four."

"So?" Felix demanded. "I'm seventy-four. You don't grow too old to fish!"

"Yes, but you've always done everything for him," Lisa explained gently. "You put the bait on the hook, you help him cast his line, you even reel it back in. Not to mention all the instructions you bark when he does try it for himself!"

"I'm just helping," Felix said, but Lisa shook her head.

"He needs to do it himself, Uncle Felix. If he did it himself, he wouldn't mind catching a small fish, or nothing at all, as you said."

✳ ✳ ✳ ✳

That night Felix thought about what Lisa had said. He supposed he did have the tendency to be a bit overbearing, he realised. He'd been fishing for so long, he considered himself to be something of an expert.

But, Felix suddenly thought, you didn't pass on a love of fishing by doing it all for the boy.

Lisa was right.

The next afternoon, Felix marched up to Warren.

"Ready to go fishing?"

Warren sighed.

"I'm sorry, Uncle Felix, but . . ."

"No buts," Felix interrupted. "We're going fishing. You and me. One

Lyme Regis, Dorset

THERE can't be many people who wouldn't immediately recognise Lyme Regis' Cobb — famous for Meryl Streep braving the storm in her cape in the film "The French Lieutenant's Woman".

It's a little bizarre that a town should be built in such an unstable place. But, despite the fact that the sea batters the coast, and the rocky shore is prone to landslip, Lyme Regis is a thriving, genteel place, where life is lived at a gentle pace.

The Cobb curves out into the sea, a grand rocky breakwater protecting the harbour, where pleasure boats bob gently.

Sailors, windsurfers and water-skiers appreciate the clean water, as do bathers on the Cobb's sandy stretch.

last time."

Warren mumbled a bit, but in the end they walked down to the rowing boat together. When they got there, however, Felix didn't take the oars like he usually did.

"You do it, Warren," he said. "I'm getting too old for this."

Surprised, Warren rowed them out on to the lake.

"Right here, by these rocks," Felix instructed. "This looks like a good spot." He stopped, looking slightly shamefaced. "That is, what do you think, Warren?"

Warren sighed.

"It's fine by me, Uncle Felix."

"You put some bait on our hooks, Warren," Felix encouraged, and Warren complied, shaking his head at his uncle.

"I know what you're trying to do, Uncle Felix, and it doesn't change a thing."

"What?" Felix barked. "What do you mean?"

"No matter how many times you let me do it," Warren explained, "whether it's rowing, baiting the hooks, casting the rods, or whatever . . . you still want to be the one doing it. I can see you're just bursting to tell me the right way to wrap a worm around the hook!"

"Well . . ." Felix shrugged, his voice gruff. "OK, but you'll learn."

They sat in the rowing boat for over an hour, silent and grim.

FELIX gazed into the still water, unhappy in his thoughts. He had always loved these afternoons, fishing with Warren in companionable silence.

He could remember when Warren was little, perhaps only five or six, leaning far over the edge of the boat.

"Do you see her, Uncle Felix?" the little boy had asked eagerly. "Do you see Molly?"

Back then, Warren had been eager to learn, to share in the excitement.

Had he spoiled it all, Felix wondered, by insisting that Warren do everything his way? He sighed, wishing that they could somehow return to those earlier, carefree days.

A jerk on his fishing line, however, brought him quickly out of his gloomy thoughts.

"Would you look at that!" he exclaimed, holding on to the rod as it began to jerk frantically. "That's no small fry, I warrant you! That's a good-sized trout!"

"Really?" Warren perked up, his face lighting up with interest. "Reel it in, Uncle Felix!"

"I can't," Felix cried, as he played the line. "This one's tough. She's hanging on. It's Molly, I think!"

The fish leapt out of the water, sparkling for a moment in the sunshine before it splashed in again, swimming back and forth and causing Felix's line to jerk viciously.

"What are you going to do?" Warren asked, fascinated, as he watched the battle between man and fish.

"I'm going to reel her in, very slowly . . ." Felix's line jerked again, and with a cry he realised he'd lost his grip on his rod.

The fishing rod he'd treasured for over forty years was yanked from his hands and landed in the water, sinking fast as the trout pulled it down in its attempt to escape.

"My rod!" Felix cried. He stared at the ripples, unable to believe his bad luck.

"I'll get it!" Without another word Warren dived into the water. Felix watched as his nephew went under again and again, searching for the fishing rod.

"Be careful!" he called out. "I don't want to lose you as well as my rod!"

Warren surfaced, grinning.

"Never fear." He held Felix's fishing rod in his hand. "We may have lost Molly, but I found your rod."

"Well done!" Felix grinned. "I've had that fishing rod for forty years. I'd have hated to lose it."

AS they rowed back to the cottage, Felix realised that, for the first time, Warren had been able to do something he, Felix, could not. And he saw that Warren realised it, too.

"Thank you, Warren," he said quietly. "You really helped me out today."

Warren shrugged, smiling.

"It's just a shame that we lost Molly."

"Never mind." Felix thought back to the sparkling scales of the proud fish, and he was almost glad she'd made her escape. "We have a great story to tell. And besides, the one that got away is always more exciting."

One had got away, Felix thought to himself, but another, more important one, had stayed.

Grinning at Warren, he knew that the day was a turning point for both of them.

"I'll tell you what," he said comfortably, as they pulled the rowing boat on to the shore, "we both still have a lot to learn about fishing!"

Warren grinned back.

"Good thing we can teach other then, isn't it, Uncle Felix?"

Felix nodded.

"Yes," he agreed. "It's a very good thing indeed!" ■

Tigger Saves The Day!

by Jenny Sandle.

"WELL, I think we should go ahead anyway. Let's cross that bridge when we come to it!"

As Maddy sat down there was a short burst of relieved applause and a murmur or two of agreement. Looking around the hall, she could see several of her neighbours nodding their heads enthusiastically.

They were at the end of an hour's meeting. It was a chilly February evening and therefore extremely hard to imagine the tiny village of Cuckfold in all its summer glory, as promised by those present.

The villagers had got together in order to decide whether they should enter this year's "Best Kept Village" competition.

Many of the visitors who passed through on their way to the coast commented on the splendid floral paradise that was summer in Cuckfold. They always showed surprise when they were told that no, the village hadn't ever won the competition. The reason was simple — they had never entered.

This year, Jan, the local postmistress, had suggested that they should give it a try, and so the meeting had been called.

Everyone had been in agreement and had put forward their plans for a bigger, better and altogether more colourful display than last year's.

The enthusiasm was infectious and things had gone splendidly — until Tom Arnold

Illustration by L. Antico.

had reminded them about Honeysuckle Cottage.

Living up to its name, Honeysuckle Cottage was smothered in swathes of rampaging honeysuckle. Granted, it looked wonderful when it was in flower, but on the down side, it was so untidy and invasive that it had swamped the house, the garden and all the paths and hedges.

FROM the main village street, all that could be seen was a mountain of untidy foliage, with a small gap cut around the gate to permit the occupant of the cottage, Rose Bennett, to make her regular outings to the shops.

"Maybe one of us could have a word with Miss Bennett?" Jan suggested.

"What about some of us going along and suggesting

73

that we do her garden for her?" Tom Arnold's son, Neil, had said. But no-one had seemed very keen on that plan.

The basic problem was that Rose Bennett was just so nice! She had a kind word for everyone in the village and was always there with help and advice if she was asked. She would babysit, take children to school, and regularly look after everyone's pets while they were away — not to mention providing tea and delicious home-baked cakes at the village fête.

Several more suggestions were made and quickly dismissed. The last thing anyone wanted to do was upset Rose. Finally, Maddy Ball's suggestion that they go ahead anyway was seized on and the meeting rapidly concluded. Surely in the months before the grand judging in July, they would have solved the problem of Rose's untidy garden!

O NLY a week later, Maddy thought that she'd stumbled on the solution. Chatting with Rose in the village shop, the conversation turned to holidays.

"I'm not sure that John and I will get away this year," she told Rose. "Perhaps we'll holiday at home for a change."

"You must try to get away, my dear. There's nothing quite like a complete change. And don't say you're worried about Harris — you know I'm more than willing to look after him. I just love that cat!" Rose smiled indulgently.

"Well, what about you?" Maddy replied, an idea suddenly popping into her head. "You never get away. You spend your summer looking after everyone else's pets. Why don't you go for a holiday?"

Maddy crossed her fingers inside her woolly mittens. If they could get Rose to go away for a few weeks, perhaps to stay with a relative, they could tidy her garden while she was absent.

"What about your sister? Doesn't she live in Torquay?"

"And what would I want with the seaside?" Rose laughed contentedly. "Nowhere suits me better than Cuckfold!" And there the conversation had ended.

* * * *

In March, they saw a glimmer of hope. Tom Arnold went to see Rose to explain that the honeysuckle spreading across the narrow pavement was becoming a nuisance.

"You see, Miss Bennett, the young mums come along here with their prams. The honeysuckle tangles the wheels and gets caught in the handles."

"Tom, I had no idea." Rose was horrified. "I'll get the hedge cut at once. You should have said before — I just didn't realise!"

Rose immediately arranged for the boys and girls of the youth club to trim the hedge, rewarding them with refreshments and a generous donation to youth club funds.

The entire village breathed a collective sigh of relief. Large pots were being sited throughout the village streets and baskets planted outside every door. Cuckfold would surpass itself this year. They were growing confident that they only needed to keep Rose Bennett's hedge neat and tidy and they would be in with a very good chance of winning the competition.

B Y May, everything was coming along splendidly. Flowers were beginning to bloom in every imaginable container and the hedge at Honeysuckle Cottage was at least controlled and looked rather nice from the outside. The judges surely wouldn't be investigating what lay behind high hedges?

Maddy was in the post office on the day that Rose Bennett walked in and dropped her bombshell. Tom Arnold had just collected his pension when Rose came through the door.

"Ah, Tom, just the person I want to see!" Rose's cheerful voice was heard clearly by everyone. "Sally Simons has just been telling me about the 'Best Kept Village' competition.

"I didn't realise we'd entered. What on earth must everyone think of me? Here they are planting and cultivating, and I'm doing nothing!" She looked around the small shop, her eyes sparkling.

"I know you all probably think I'm too old to bother, but I would like to do something."

Everyone smiled at each other. Their luck had changed! They were hugging themselves with the thought that the one blot on their landscape would disappear when Rose's next words withered their joy as thoroughly as a June frost.

"So, Tom, I'd like you to get your young folk round again. They've been doing a splendid job of keeping the pavement clear. I'd like them to cut down my hedge to about four feet. We'll lose some of the flowers, but at least the judges will be able to see into my garden.

"The honeysuckle will be a marvellous sight by July, and with my garden where it is, the judges will see it right from the other end of the street! It'll be an explosion of colour and perfume and it'll knock them for six! So, bring the workforce around as soon as you can!"

And, bidding her stunned audience a jolly "good morning", Rose was gone.

It was some minutes before anyone could say anything, and then they all spoke at once. Sadly, no-one could see how Tom could get out of it. Confident expectations were squashed, and they could all visualise the coveted award slipping from their reach.

And so the honeysuckle hedge was taken down to four feet. The youth club funds benefited enormously, but a blight was put on the entire village by the messy jumble that was exposed.

Now that the hedge had gone, they could see that the honeysuckle had twined and strangled its way through everything. All that could be seen was a huge green jungle, buds ready to burst into life.

In the middle of the riot of foliage stood the cottage itself. In contrast to the chaos around it, the building was neat and orderly, as though disassociating itself from the confusion surrounding it.

Several people put forward suggestions as to how they might disguise the plot or distract the judges, but none was really practical. Besides, Rose Bennett was delighted, convinced that the sight of her "honeysuckle carpet" would win Cuckfold the much-yearned-for trophy.

AND that was when Tigger took a hand . . .

It would be more correct to say that Tigger took a paw, for Tigger was Rose Bennett's large fluffy cat. He was ten years old and well used to the traffic that drove rather too fast down the village street. In spite of parading about tail in the air, as though he was lord of the manor, he would scuttle out of the way when a car came along. Unfortunately, one day he wasn't quite quick enough.

Maddy received a distraught telephone call from Rose.

"Oh, Maddy! Thank goodness you're home." Rose sounded panicky. "It's Tigger. I heard a squeal of brakes and Tigger came limping through the gate. I think his leg may be broken!"

"Don't fret, Rose. I'll get the car out and be round in a moment. We'll have Tigger off to the vet and fixed up before you know it!"

"No, no, you don't understand. I went to fetch him and he ran away from me – he's taken refuge right in the middle of the garden.

"There used to be a miniature wishing well there and my beautiful honeysuckle carpet has covered it. Tigger is underneath all that and I can't get to him!" Her words ended in a wail and Maddy promised to get hold of Tom Arnold and come immediately.

* * * *

"Oh, Maddy, can you hear him?" Rose cried.

Poor Tigger was somewhere under the thick mat of foliage and flowers, miaowing quietly. Rose tried to coax him out, tapping a fork against a food tin, making welcoming noises, even miaowing herself, all to no avail.

Tom tried shaking at the honeysuckle in an attempt to move Tigger, but the cat stayed firmly where he was. Rose was becoming more and more distraught.

"There's nothing else for it, Tom," she said at last. "You'll have to cut a

The Return

THE time passed, and to Kate's delight
  Her Joe returned at last,
So happy to be home again,
Their separation past.

With Joe now nicely settled
And his future prospects clear,
He and Kate decided they
Could maybe wed next year.

The time had come for Kate and Joe
To plan for married life
By searching for a modest home
To suit a man and wife.

They found a cosy little place
And furnished it with care;
A small but perfect haven
For a newly-married pair.

— *Alice Drury.*

way through to him. Tigger must get to the vet, and I'm afraid the village will just have to understand if I ruin my glorious honeysuckle carpet. After all, an animal's welfare is far more important than a trophy!"

It took less than half an hour to cut a swathe through the honeysuckle. By mid-afternoon, Tigger was recuperating at the local vet's surgery. He would be allowed home in the morning, splinted but otherwise well.

When they returned to the cottage, Rose surveyed her garden and turned a tearful face to Maddy.

"Oh, Maddy, look at the mess. My garden will spoil the entire village. What can we do about it?"

* * * *

The judging was held on a perfect summer day. The panel of judges went from house to house along the street, noting their comments in little notebooks.

They were highly entertained by the ancient petrol pump now brightly painted and brought in to serve as a basket hanger! They loved the traditional stone horse trough and applauded the enterprise of those who had filled jam pans and copper kettles with glorious summer flowers and hung them outside their cottages.

When they arrived at Honeysuckle Cottage, however, they stood and looked for almost five full minutes before asking if they could enter and look around.

When the entire population of the village had set to in order to "salvage" Rose's garden they had soon uncovered and then restored the original features.

By the time they'd finished, the wishing well stood in the centre, surrounded by a formal rose garden. A pergola, hung with sweet-scented honeysuckle, let the way around the side and back of the cottage. Large beds of bright bedding plants were separated by gravel paths, and tubs and pots provided colour and height.

At the side of the garden, a small fountain trickled into a sparkling pond. The cat sitting next to the pond looked like an ornament, but as the judges approached he ran off towards the back of the cottage where a neat kitchen garden boasted lettuces, marrows and anything else that Tom Arnold had thought would be up and growing by the day of the judging.

* * * *

Many years later, Maddy took her small grandchildren for a walk down the village street. Outside Honeysuckle Cottage, she stopped to point out the small statue of a very contented cat, snoozing next to a plaque proudly proclaiming the annual success of Cuckfold in the "Best Kept Village" competition. ∎

Illustration by Ben Warner.

I
T'S so far . . ."
"Where?"
Daisy suddenly turned,
unaware she had spoken
aloud. The orderly held the
costume midway between
the basket and the rack,
his head on one side.
Fingering the beading
on the georgette dress,
she wasn't all that sure
she wanted to explain.

"Eternity," she said
softly.

"Oh." He continued
hanging up the clothes.

Brief Encounter

by Sue
Burbage.

"Yes, it is a long way. Have you been
there?"

His grin eased the tension and she
smiled back. At every camp there were
always helpers, but the uniform
camouflaged the individual.

The grin broadened and he spoke
lightly, as though it were a joke.

"I don't really expect an answer."

For a moment Daisy was struck by
the rare whiteness of his teeth, but
they were eclipsed by the brilliance of
his eyes.

She blushed, stammering an apology.

"It was rude of me to stare. But . . ."
Daisy hastily bent, rummaging in the basket

79

as though searching for something.

"Don't tell me . . . I remind you of someone?"

Almost every person in every camp came from somewhere different; Britain could be mapped a dozen times over in every barracks.

She nodded, still unable to look at him.

The moss-green eyes flecked with brown returned her momentarily to the woods, and James. It had been so long, so very long since she'd seen him, and a month since his last letter. Perhaps . . .

The horrible thought made her quickly close her eyes. No. She would have heard if anything . . .

The man's voice broke into her thoughts.

"'Ere, let me." He took the armful of clothes from her. "Where is he?"

"He's . . . he's a long way away — an eternity away. In the RAF."

The orderly was roughly the same height as James but had thick, sandy hair instead of her boyfriend's tousled dark brown. But his friendliness was inviting and she found herself talking.

"There, that's done. What's next?"

Daisy was about to answer when Lotty, the other female in the troupe, tapped her on the shoulder.

"Tea's up. In the office!"

JOINING the rest of her colleagues, Daisy noticed the orderly had vanished.

Lotty nudged her arm.

"Some right smashers in this lot! You had a nice one helping you!"

"Lotty, you know I can't, not with James . . ."

"Come off it. It's only a bit of harmless fun — nothing wrong in a bit of chat and company. Everyone needs someone to talk to . . . even you."

Her words hovered in the air. Lotty believed in enjoying herself and flirted at every opportunity, and she was always trying to entice her friend to follow suit.

As Daisy finished her tea, the thought lingered temptingly for the first time.

The show opened with Daisy singing a sprightly number. By the second chorus, feet were tapping and hands clapping, and Daisy had to make a concerted effort not to look at the orderly standing in the far corner. As she finished he cheered and whistled shrilly with the others.

The show was a success. Lotty and Daisy received the greatest applause and, after the National Anthem, they were besieged, until they steadily retreated, smiling their thanks, to the small office.

"Phew — that went well," Daisy said, as they changed.

Lotty preened herself in the tiny mirror and gave a giggle.

"Did you see him? The tall, dark, good-looking one with the cheeky grin — second row, third on the left!"

Daisy laughed.

"Lotty, you are a terror!"

"How else am I going to find my knight in shining armour, ducky?" Buttoning her jacket and smoothing her skirt, Lotty momentarily cringed.

"Ugh! These uniforms are awful — they do nothing for the figure. Perhaps I could shorten it an inch or two . . ." She raised the material above her knees.

"You know it's not allowed!"

"I know." Lotty sighed. "Just wishful thinking."

Holding the mirror up once more, she added another layer to her already scarlet lips.

"I know I keep saying it, ducky, but it's about time you relaxed and enjoyed yourself a bit. This war's a lonely business and the men appreciate a little attention. Life can be all too short nowadays." She linked an arm in Daisy's.

"Come on, let's go and get some grub."

The lights from the mess hall stretched between the huts like distorted stepping-stones, and a thin mist had begun to settle between the buildings. They were grateful to get out of the damp and into the warmth of the noisy hall.

They found the other entertainers already eating and chatting with the regulars and, just as Daisy sat down, a plate of mash and Spam was placed in front of her. Looking up, she saw it had been put there by the orderly. He smiled, then, much to her surprise, sat beside her.

"Don't let me stop you . . ." He indicated her meal.

He didn't speak until she had finished eating and there was a lull in the conversation around the table.

"I enjoyed the show. We all did. You were —" his finger traced a crack in the table "— wonderful."

Pushing the plate away, Daisy could feel her heartbeat increase.

HIS voice was soothing as the noise around them faded. Daisy felt herself look directly at him, despite the warnings in her head. His name was Ray and he was a long way from home, like everyone else. She suspected he had someone, somewhere, but it wasn't the time to ask. The war had a way of turning principles upside down.

They walked between the tables and out into the night. The mist was thicker, making them anonymous. On the way back to her hut they strolled side by side. Daisy wondered what it would be like to slip her hand into his and for their arms to touch.

"Have you heard the one about Hitler and the hedgehog?"

At the end of the joke they both laughed, and he took her hand. It was warm and a little rough, but the feeling tingled all the way up her arm.

As they reached the hut she heard Lotty call from behind. Her friend came running breathlessly out of the shadows.

"Daisy! Just after you left, Sarge brought the mail. It was delayed — only just caught us up. There was a letter for you."

Daisy took the small white envelope, recognising James's writing.

Lotty winked as she left, linking her arm with the man from the second row, third on the left, who smiled smugly.

Daisy slipped the letter into her top pocket and leaned against the door. Ray stood to one side, his arm resting slightly above her head.

He moved closer. He was talking — she'd almost forgotten what it was like to have someone so near they only needed to whisper . . .

She felt James's letter lying heavily in her pocket.

Wasn't it only a piece of paper?

"I'd better go. We've another performance in the morning," she faltered.

"Yes." But instead of moving away, he drew closer.

Daisy could see every detail of his face; she wanted to sweep away the fringe that threatened to obscure his eyes, to have his lips touch hers . . .

"You're right." He suddenly stepped back, startling her. "I've got breakfast to prepare. Up at five-thirty."

Her breath caught in her throat and she could only nod.

"Goodnight, then," he whispered, retreating into the mist.

She closed her eyes in relief, and sorrow.

RAY met Daisy in the mess hall for breakfast. Lotty, too, was chaperoned and, for their brief time together, before the second and final performance, they laughed and joked as though out on a double date.

Later, as the hall filled up again, Ray took up the same viewing position in the corner. After the show he helped dismantle the stage and reload the lorry.

Guilt had prevented Daisy from opening James's letter the previous evening, but now, in the quiet of the empty office, she took it out.

He told of the endless card and cricket games, and books read to fill the hours of waiting between each call. He told of the paralysis when the bell rang to scramble and the rush as instinct took over. He spoke of the losses — mainly the young and inexperienced boys. Too young, he said, too enthusiastic.

His letter finished by asking about her and the shows, and when they could see each other again . . .

When she looked up from the letter, Ray was standing in front of her.

"All's aboard!" He thrust his hands in his pockets. "Thought I'd find you here. Is he OK?"

"Just."

He nodded.

"I can understand that. So, where to next?"

She shrugged.

"Back to HQ and then orders for somewhere else. We never know where."

He nodded, taking another step towards her.

"You see . . . eternity is nearer than you think." Out of his pocket he pulled an envelope. "It's a small world — though sometimes the miles seem to stretch to infinity. But these . . ." he fingered the creased paper " . . . bring it closer."

"Yes." She smiled. He was a nice man, and a good one.

He leaned forward and lightly kissed her on the lips.

"Good luck."

"And you." Daisy hesitated in the doorway. "She's a lucky woman. I hope you'll see each other soon."

She knew and Ray knew that they would never meet again — but each would always hold a small corner of the other's heart.

Daisy straightened her back and climbed aboard the lorry, bound for an unknown destination. ∎

Don't Miss Your "Friend" Every Week!

IF you've enjoyed this Annual, you'll love "The People's Friend" magazine. It has something for everyone! It's full of exciting serials and heartwarming, romantic stories.

We've got it covered if you're into craft, knitting, cookery or gardening, and there are also regular features on Britain's beauty spots — whether in London or on a deserted Scottish island.

And don't forget our competitions, offers, letters and snaps, doctor's column and evocative poetry. There's even a special Children's Corner!

If you'd like to know more, ask your newsagent about our subscription rates, or write to: Subscribers Dept., "The People's Friend", 80 Kingsway East, Dundee DD4 8SL.

J ENNIE buried her nose into the bunch of sweet peas and drew in a
long, deep breath, letting the rich, heavenly scent carry her away
from reality for a few seconds. With their long, slender stems and
delicate pink, white and blue bonnets, they were undoubtedly her
favourite flowers.

She could so easily keep this bunch and enjoy it, she told herself. But
today of all days, perhaps she could put it to some better use . . .

Her heart had felt heavy this morning as she'd watched the removal
van reverse up her neighbour's drive. With a hiss of air brakes it had
come to rest beside the lilac tree she remembered Jack and Mary planting

Illustration by Sally Rowe.

Time To Move On

by Julia Courtney.

many years ago. Mary and her son, David, came out to meet the removal men.

Peeling off her rubber gloves, Jennie had hurried to the front door.

"Let me know if there's anything I can do," she'd called across to her neighbours. "Maybe a cup of tea and some sandwiches before you go?"

"Thanks, Jennie," David said. "I'm sure we'll need it by the time all this lot's packed." He'd given Jennie an understanding smile. Of course, it was the end of an era for him, too, she'd thought sadly.

"Well, that's what neighbours are for, you know," Jennie had told him, blinking back her tears. She'd had to hurry back indoors before she started crying and made a fool of herself.

"Sounds like the removal men have arrived," Keith announced a few minutes later, as he came into the kitchen from the garden. He had taken off his wellingtons and was standing beside her in his socks.

"Yes," Jennie said wistfully, as she took the bunch of sweet peas that he was holding out to her.

"It was about this time of the year when we moved in, wasn't it?" he said.

"And Mary and Jack came round to introduce themselves." Jennie nodded. "Do you remember? Mary brought me some flowers from her garden."

SHE remembered seeing Mary's friendly smile for the first time.

"I'm Mary Anderson, from next door," she'd said.

"Our garden still looked like a builder's yard." Jennie allowed herself a little giggle. "It was such a kind thought."

"And the beginning of a long friendship," Keith added. "David was still in a pushchair, and they hadn't even had Paul and Sally, then." A smile crossed his face as he recalled those long-ago days.

"Our Sadie and Tom had just started at nursery." Jennie, too, let her mind slip back over the years. She pictured the children racing up and down the pavement on their tricycles.

"Oh, Keith — I'm going to miss Mary so much. Why does she have to move so far away?"

"It makes sense, love. You know it does." Keith put a loving arm around Jennie's shoulders. "From what she's told us, David has a big house, and he's had the go-ahead to build a granny annexe. She'll be able to see more of Paul, too — and her sister and the grandchildren. And don't forget, it's where she grew up. It's not as if she's going off to some place she doesn't know."

Jennie swallowed hard. She knew Keith was right. Mary had never learned to drive, and the journey to visit her family could take almost all day on public transport. Mary had explained that she couldn't expect David and Paul to come running after her all the time, and it was even harder for Sally, who lived abroad.

"In any case, Mary's house is far too big for her now. It was even too big for them when Jack was still alive, and the children had left home," Keith said.

Jennie smiled.

"Do you remember when they only had those two bedrooms and a boxroom?"

"And then the builders came," Keith put in, with a smile.

"They added that porch on the back so the children had somewhere to put their wellingtons," Jennie reminded him. "I thought it was such a good idea that I persuaded you that we should do the same thing a year later."

"And now they have that huge kitchen, and four bedrooms . . . and a conservatory," Keith went on.

"They didn't want to move. Their house was like Topsy . . . it just growed and growed." Jennie found herself letting out a little chuckle. "A bit like ours, really."

Still smiling, she made up her mind to give the sweet peas to Mary. She found a small vase, twisted some foil around the stems and put the flowers into water.

L OOKING out across the long lawn which ran down to the pavement, Jennie noticed how much all the shrubs had grown, too, over the years. It was hard to picture what the estate had been like when they'd first moved into their house. Most of the gardens had been bare and exposed, and many plots had still been full of builder's rubble.

But now, the gardens in Lawrence Drive were bordered with mature trees and hedges, and many of the houses had been drastically altered from their original design. Most of them had changed ownership several times, too, over the years. But Jennie and Mary had been neighbours for ever . . . or so it seemed.

"The children have grown up, too," Keith reminded Jennie, breaking into her quiet thoughts. "Do you remember when Sadie and Tom used to play on that swing in Mary's garden?" he said, picking up a tea towel as she turned back to the washing up.

"And Mary's three used to come into our garden and splash with our two in the paddling pool . . ."

The old swing was still there, the chains a bit rusty now, and the plastic seat more often than not covered with dead leaves from the overhanging tree. But Mary had kept the swing for the day that she and Jack would have grandchildren to use it.

Tears rushed back into Jennie's eyes as she recalled those long summer days when their children had been young. She could almost hear the squeals and the laughter when Keith had put the hose on the children and the boys had chased the girls around the lawn in a state of wild excitement. What hours of fun they'd all had together.

Those were memories that could never be taken away, Jennie reminded herself.

"And what about those days when we rigged up that tent in our garden and all the children had their tea out there?" she said with a wistful smile.

"Tom and David had just joined the Boy Scouts," Keith recalled. "Wasn't that when they were in their wild Africa period? They were always pretending to be on safari.

"Remember that day they cooked sausages over that campfire?" He chuckled. "Burnt to a cinder on the outside they were . . ."

BROUGHTY

A residential suburb of Dundee and a holiday resort with a sandy beach facing towards Fife, Broughty Ferry was once wealthier than any other town of a corresponding size in Scotland.

This, of course, was thanks to the jute trade. The owners of the mills set up home near their works, and yet far enough away to distance themselves.

Broughty Ferry also boasts a castle, a battlemented oblong structure erected about the beginning of the 16th century. It's open to the public today, so you can enjoy a holiday and a history lesson all in one in this delightful seaside town!

"And raw on the inside," Jennie finished for him, chuckling. "To think Tom went in for catering at college," she added.

"They've all done well for themselves," Keith said. "They've done both our families proud."

"They were good times."

"And there'll be more good times," Keith said firmly.

"Perhaps," Jennie said, trying to convince herself. She couldn't begin to think of her home without Mary next door.

She finished washing up and wiped down the draining board, squeezing out the cloth more vigorously than usual.

"It's all right for the one who's going — it's the ones left behind who suffer," she said.

She was angry with herself that she hadn't yet been able to accept Mary's move. What was the matter with her? It wasn't as if the news had been sprung upon them suddenly.

Ever since Jack had died six months ago, Mary had taken to coming round to Jennie's, having consoling cups of tea and hinting at the fact that David thought the move would be for the best. But when the time came,

FERRY *Dundee*

Spectrum Colour Library.

and Mary told Jennie that the house was on the market and she'd made up her mind to go, Jennie hadn't been able to disguise the fact that she'd felt slightly hurt.

Jennie glanced out of the window — just in time to see the men carrying a bed into the van. She shivered. She couldn't bear to look.

Switching on the radio, she tuned in to some lively music. Suddenly, a smile spread across her face. They were playing that familiar tune that had always been used at their keep-fit classes!

I T had been Mary's idea for them both to join the group, about twelve years ago.

"Come on, Jen!" she'd said, "Let's got for it!"

"But look at me!" Jennie had countered. "I'd look ridiculous in a leotard!"

"You can wear jogging pants, or trousers, like I'm going to do," Mary had said.

Jennie grinned as she recalled going into that first class, wearing her black linen trousers, feeling very unfit and more than a little overweight. She and Mary had tried to keep to the back of the room, struggling with their skipping ropes and trying to spin their hoops around their waists. Even now, she found it hard to believe how much they'd puffed and panted at such simple exercise.

Now, she automatically found herself side-stepping in the kitchen in time to the music.

Her mind drifted on. One thing had led to another. She'd become more and more interested in keeping fit until, one day, she'd been asked to start an exercise class for older women. Only this morning, someone had rung her up to ask if she was going to be continuing with the class next term — and of course, she was.

It was a very worthwhile interest, she realised — and it had really all been thanks to Mary. What a lovely legacy she was leaving behind.

* * * *

"Can I help get the lunch?" Keith asked, a few hours later.

Jennie gasped. She hadn't realised how quickly the time had flown. Together, she and Keith rustled up a plate of cold meat and salad sandwiches fit for a king.

A little later, she heard that familiar tapping on the back door.

"May we come in?" Mary peeped into the kitchen.

"Of course," Jennie said, trying to force a lighter tone into her voice. "You must both be worn out. Come and sit down."

As she filled the kettle, she watched the removal men closing the van doors.

"I'm going to miss you," Jennie said, as they heard the van start up.

"It's for the best, you know." Mary's pleading eyes met Jennie's. "And we'll keep in touch, won't we?"

"Of course we will," Jennie replied, trying to smile. "What about if we agree to meet once a week in Woodchester?" she said, on impulse. "Perhaps we could have lunch together?"

"What a good idea! And once I'm settled in, maybe I'll start up a keep-fit class for older women — like you did." Mary's eyes sparkled mischievously. "You could be one of my first students!"

The two women laughed as they'd done so often, and reached to hold hands across the table. Then Jennie pulled out her hanky and blew her nose.

"I do hope everything will work out all right for you," she said.

"I'm sure it will." Mary sounded positive. "David's a good lad."

He was, Jennie thought. But even so, she could see now that it couldn't be any easier for Mary than it was for her. In an ideal world, Jack would be alive and they'd both still be living next door.

"Nothing stays the same for ever," Jennie said, putting on a brave smile. She knew she had to be thankful for all the good times they'd had together. "But your house just won't seem the same any more without you there."

"It'll come to life again. The young couple who are moving in — the Morrisons — they're just about the same age as we were when we arrived, and they have two small children."

"Don't tell me we'll be putting up tents again!" Keith said, in mock horror.

"And cooking sausages!" Mary joined in Keith's laughter.

"Thanks for everything," Mary said as she stood up to leave. With tears in her eyes, she gave Jenny a good hug. "We're not going to lose touch. Not after all this time."

"Take care," Jennie whispered, holding her tightly. "I'll see you soon." Then, suddenly swept up with the urgency and emotion of them going, she and Keith followed Mary and David out to their car.

It was only after the car was out of sight that Jennie remembered the flowers.

"The sweet peas! They're still in the kitchen. I forgot to give them to Mary," she said, as the loss of her friend began to sweep over her like a cool breeze.

"Never mind," Keith said, putting his arm around her. "You can enjoy them yourself."

L ATER that afternoon, the Morrisons' removal van arrived. Jennie heard the sound of children's excited voices as they ran in and out of the house, watching the removal men bringing in their furniture and belongings. The rain, which had been threatening all day, had passed over, and as the removal men finally drove off, Jennie spotted some patches of blue in the sky.

She let out a nervous sigh. Now — it was time to introduce herself, she thought, and to welcome her new neighbours, just as Mary had welcomed her and Keith all those years ago.

The couple next door were just like they had been once, she thought, as she opened the front door. And it was going to be nice having the sound of children's laughter around the place once more.

"Hello," she said, holding out the bunch of sweet peas as her new young neighbour opened the door. "I'm Jennie McDonald from next door."

And as Ailsa Morrison smiled in surprise and gratefully accepted the flowers, Jennie knew that she'd done the right thing. ∎

A Perfect S

IS that Sarah, Nina?"
I look out of the window. A taxi draws up outside, but it's for Annie Marshall across the lane. She's going to do her weekly shopping.

"No, Dad, it's Annie's taxi."

"I should have gone with Matt and helped with the luggage."

"Dad, you've just had an operation. You can't lift anything!"

"Sarah may be expecting to see me at the airport," he continues, frowning. "I should have gone."

"Dad, she knows about the operation and won't expect you there."

It's been four years since we last saw my sister. She's a naturalist who has travelled all over the world and now lives in Australia.

"Shouldn't they be here by now?"

"It's too early. She has to clear Customs and —"

I let it go. The workings of an airport are a mystery to Dad. Although I would have loved to go with my husband to meet Sarah off the plane, running a "holiday inn" for cats and dogs makes getting away difficult.

"Mum," Kimberley shouts from the kitchen, "Domino's been sick again!"

Domino is one of my "regular" cats and it's time for her medication.

The accommodation for the animals is new and was built by Dad and Matt. Matt is one of the few men I know who is happy to live near his father-in-law. He calls Dad "the salt of the earth" — and he is.

A retired cabinetmaker, he now carves pieces from driftwood as a hobby and has built up quite a reputation. He calls a spade a spade and is brilliant in a crisis — but not today. Because today, his favourite daughter is coming home.

A PLANE flying overhead causes me to look up. I wonder if it is the flight carrying Sarah, and a frisson of excitement runs through me.

Always "the pretty one", my sister could have married many times over, but chose travel and a career instead. She is the day to my night, and I can hardly wait to see her.

After giving Domino her medicine, I make some tea and take Dad a cup — but I can't find him.

"He's out in the garden talking to some man." Kimberley flops down on the settee with a sigh. She hates having to give up her room for her aunt.

ster

by
Mhairi
Grant.

Illustration by John Hancock.

93

"Have you taken those posters down and left everything tidy?" I ask.

"Ye-es," she replies with a roll of her eyes, " although I still don't see why she couldn't go into Mark's room. After all . . ."

But I'm not listening. Her brother will be coming home from university in two days and he needs a place to study. I wander out into the garden.

"Sarah has even made a study of the mountain gorillas in Rwanda and appeared on television in Australia and the States . . ." I hear Dad say.

He's normally a man of few words, but if Sarah is his chosen subject he can easily talk for ten minutes without taking a breath. The whole village knows of her impending visit — including any passers-by. The man, who is out walking his dog, looks over at me.

"Oh, and this is my other daughter, Nina."

"Pleased to meet you," the man says politely. "And what do you do?"

"I run a boarding kennel," I reply, looking up at the sign.

It doesn't sound as exciting as studying mountain gorillas, but then again I'm not my sister.

"Nina's more of a homebody, like me," Dad explains.

THAT'S true, but I wish I were like my dad in other ways, too. He is so well respected in the village that all the neighbours come to him for advice. Even Matt has been known to disappear for hours on end to the local pub with my dad and come back waxing lyrical about "the father I never had".

But I'm quite shy and reserved and it takes time for me to get to know people. Mum was the same. When she died it came as a shock to everyone as she'd refused to let anyone know that she'd been ill.

We exchange a few more polite words before going back into the house. Dad refuses to sit down and paces the floor.

Unable to help him, I go into Kimberley's room to double check that everything is in order. She has left her diary open next to her computer. I try not to look but can't help but notice the words, *AUNT SARAH COMING TODAY*, in big bold letters. It reminds me of Dad's scrapbook.

In it he has photographs and newspaper cuttings of all Sarah's achievements. I'm sure Mum started it, but Dad has kept it up. He never mentions it, but I came across it recently when I was looking for clean pyjamas to take into the hospital for him.

His pride in Sarah is evident in the way everything is catalogued and dated. It makes me wish that I could do something that would make him proud of me.

Unable to sit still, I go out to the animals. The dogs and cats appreciate the extra attention and listen to every word I tell them about my sister. Silly, I know, but I make a habit of speaking to my charges. I'm still

The Wedding

WHEN Kate and Joe got married
The village church was full –
With members of the family
And friends from work and school.

As Joe, the handsome bridegroom,
Stood waiting for his bride,
He saw her coming up the aisle
And felt a glow of pride.

She looked a perfect picture
In her gown of silk and lace,
With a spray of orange blossom
On the veil around her face.

She joined him at the altar
And stood there by his side.
The vicar gave his blessings
And the marriage knot was tied.

– *Alice Drury.*

nattering away when Kimberley comes running out.

"They're here!"

Dad's eyes are bright with excitement and his hands shake. For his sake I affect a calm I don't feel.

As Sarah gets out of the car, I let Dad greet her first. Tears spring to his eyes as he hugs her. Then it's my turn. The years fall away as we reclaim our childhood, laughing and hugging. Words punctuate our excitement, as sentences remain unfinished.

"You're bound to be tired. Go and have a lie down while I put the dinner on," I urge.

"Oh, no, Nina," Sarah protests. "I'm dying to see the new accommodation for all your boarders. Dad tells me that it's very posh, and that you and Matt have worked like Trojans to get it set up."

"He told you that?"

"Of course, that's all he ever writes about — how well you've done." She grimaces and then grins, meaning no offence. "He's even sent me photos of the construction of the pet houses and details of the plans. He says that your customers are delighted with the care that their pets get and that it's the best boarding kennel in the country."

I grin, too.

"I think he's exaggerating."

"No, I'm not," Dad says, putting his arms round our shoulders. "Come on, I'll give you a guided tour."

MATT winks at me as I'm drawn along, listening to Dad tell Sarah all about my business. He talks with an enthusiastic knowledge and . . . pride.

"Keeps me young, it does, helping Nina out now and again . . ."

He squeezes my arm and then stops.

"Listen to me, chattering like an old woman. But I'll hold my peace now."

Sarah catches my eye and smiles mischievously.

"What? Before you tell me all about Nina's family?"

"Well . . . I did tell you about Mark passing his first year exams, didn't I, and Matt's promotion at work?"

"At least four times."

"Oh, and Kimberley is going to be the Rose Queen at this year's pageant."

Sarah laughs, while I listen to Dad in astonishment.

"But best of all," Dad says gruffly, "I've got my two lovely girls together again. What more can a man ask for?"

I resolve to dig out that old scrapbook later. I have a feeling Sarah might like to see it . . . ■

by Shirley Worrall.

Illustration by David Young.

COMING HOME

S ARAH couldn't resist a quick peep at the cottage. It was empty,
so who was to know? Besides, she reasoned, as soon as a *For Sale*
board went up in the front garden, it was as good as offering Joe
Public an invitation to trespass.

Not that a *For Sale* board would do much good here. The cottage was
so far off the beaten track that no-one would spot it unless, like her,
they'd come here specially to see it again.

The cottage had been named The Retreat, and Sarah had first seen it
— and fallen in love with it — at four years of age.

"The garden's a mountain!" she'd told her parents, the words tripping
over themselves in her excitement.

That had been twenty-three years ago.

They'd come here on holiday every year — Sarah, her parents, and her
brothers Joe, Mark, Andrew and Harry — until she was sixteen. Then,
more exotic destinations·had beckoned — not that Sarah had found them
more exotic . . .

"But can't we go to Exmoor?" she'd wailed.

"We're going to Italy," her mum had replied, laughing at such an
absurd suggestion. "It's too cold in Exmoor, and there's too much rain."

Sarah could never remember it raining, or being cold . . .

Pushing her memories aside, she opened the gate at the front and
stepped into the garden. The old tree was still standing, the one which
had been so many things in their childhood games — a house, a boat, a

97

castle, a jungle.

It was, she decided as she looked around, her favourite place in the world.

She'd had holidays in Spain, Greece, France and Italy, but nothing could compete with The Retreat. She loved it.

If only The Retreat were hers. She'd love to get the garden back into shape.

Some chance of that, she thought ruefully.

Anyway, she'd had enough of house-hunting over the last three months. She'd come here to get away from all that — and from Mike.

But she wasn't going to think about him, she told herself firmly.

No, she'd come to Exmoor for a holiday.

All the same, her thoughts went on, it wouldn't hurt to phone the estate agents and see how much they were asking for The Retreat . . .

S HE made her way round to the back of the cottage but, instead of seeing an expanse of rough moorland, as expected, she collided with what, for a moment, felt like a wall. But the obstacle was warmer and not quite as unforgiving as the old stonework.

"I'm terribly sorry," the man said, stepping back from her. "I didn't realise anyone was here."

"Oh!" She started in fright. "I didn't either."

Once she'd got her breath back, Sarah took a good look at him. Average height, but nearly as solidly built as the cottage. Dark hair. An almost guarded expression. Blue jacket over a white T-shirt.

Apart from the guarded expression, he wasn't bad looking.

Not that she was interested, she reminded herself sharply. She'd come on holiday to escape so-called romance — she certainly wasn't looking for a man.

"Nice place," he said, nodding at the cottage.

"Beautiful," she agreed.

"You're — er, just viewing then?"

She realised then why he'd looked so guilty. Like her, he was merely snooping.

"Yes, just viewing," she said. "You?"

"The same. Do you have the key?"

"No. Do you?"

"No." He smiled, and the expression was gone. "I knew there was no point as soon as I saw the asking price. Like you, I'm trespassing."

"We're hardly trespassing," she answered, cringing a little as she remembered that same word flitting through her mind. "Surely the whole point of the agent's board is to get people looking?"

"Hmmm." Clearly he wasn't convinced.

"So what is the asking price?"

He reached into the back pocket of his jeans, and pulled out the folded details.

"Here. See for yourself."

The price, in bold black print, leaped off the page.

"Never!" she gasped.

"'Fraid so," he said, his gaze returning to the cottage. "Nice place, though."

"Yes, but even so, I can't see it selling for that much." But perhaps it would. If the last three months had taught her anything, it was that house prices were crazy these days.

"It's gorgeous inside," she went on. "Lots of nooks and crannies."

"I know." He nodded, smiling. "I used to spend summer holidays here."

"Really? What a coincidence. So did I, with Mum and Dad and my four brothers."

"I came with Mum, Dad and two sisters," he said, laughing. "We always came at the same time — the first two weeks of the school holidays."

Sarah laughed.

"We always came for the last two weeks," she explained, "because Mum thought it was something for us to look forward to."

"My mum said we'd be unbearable if we had to wait that long," he told her with amusement.

AND then, regrettably, it seemed as if they'd run out of conversation.

"I'd better be off," she said after a long silence.

"Me, too."

They walked to the front of the property.

"You don't have a car," she remarked. "Can I give you a lift somewhere?"

"Thanks, but my car's only at the top of the track." He shuffled his feet awkwardly. "I was going to walk to the pub. Fancy coming along?"

"The Smuggler?" she asked, and he nodded.

"Gosh!" She had to laugh. "I spent hours there — drinking lemonade, eating crisps, and playing with their rabbit."

"Blue," he said, naming the rabbit, and Sarah's eyes widened in amazement.

"Yes! You knew him, too?"

"So would you like to come?" he asked again. "Blue's long gone, as have his owners, but they do good lunches. We can sit in the garden and — oh, I'm Ian Taylor, by the way."

"Sarah. Sarah Jennings."

The Smuggler hadn't changed much over the years.

"They used to have a tree house," Sarah remarked, tucking into her scampi. "Remember that?"

"Yes. I expect it had to go — one of these new Health and Safety regulations."

"I expect so. What a shame, though. That new climbing stuff —" she nodded to the children's play area "— doesn't look nearly so much fun."

"No."

Sarah couldn't believe this. It was if their whole lives had been lived along parallel lines . . .

HOW long are you staying?" she asked, assuming that he, like her, was on holiday.

"I live here," he replied.

"Oh, lucky you!"

"Yes." He smiled at that. "I run my own computer consultancy business, so I can work more or less anywhere. I moved here six years ago.

"For most of that time," he added with a grimace, "I've been looking for a nice house to buy. When I saw The Retreat advertised, I couldn't believe my luck. But at that price, it's well out of my range."

"And mine. I've been looking for something rural — though not here," she added quickly. "I live in Exeter. I'm only here for a fortnight's holiday. I've got a flat in town and I've been looking for something in one of the villages for months now. But they're all either too expensive, or falling down."

He nodded in understanding.

"Until I saw the board in the garden at The Retreat, I hadn't thought of moving up here. I could, though," she murmured, and her heart began to race with excitement.

"I work from home, too," she explained. "I'm a photographer. Well, mostly I work from home. I do two days in a studio — portraits of babies, mainly — to help pay the mortgage."

But there was nothing to stop her moving here, she realised suddenly. She would only be a few hours' drive from her family. And without Mike to think about —

"Are there any decent cheap properties around here?" she asked eagerly, and he laughed.

"None that I've found!"

Her heart sank. As usual, she was being too impulsive. She could almost hear Mike's wholehearted agreement.

Mike was ambitious, always planning for the future. He worked in sales, and was obsessed — Sarah's word — with targets and budgets,

Edzell Castle

EDZELL lies a few miles north of Brechin, close to the right bank of the North Esk. Edzell's real claim to fame, however, is a mile west of the village — Edzell Castle.

In 1604, Sir David Lindsay turned his thoughts to the grounds around his castle. In those days only the wealthy could afford the luxury of a designed garden — very much a symbol of power and success.

Today, the parterre has been recreated to breathe life back into the beautiful gardens of the family affectionately known as the Lichtsome Lindsays.

A visit here would lighten anybody's heart — and inspire the most reluctant gardener!

bonuses and commissions.

"You ought to buy one of those places on the new estate," he'd told her.

"But I don't want to live on an estate."

"It would be an investment, Sarah," he'd pointed out with as much patience as he could muster.

"I don't want an investment," she'd cried. "I want a home!"

Sarah lived for the day; Mike planned for the future. In the end, they'd both despaired of each other, and had gone their separate ways.

"Are you here on your own?" Ian broke into her thoughts.

"Yes." She felt herself colour, and thought he must be able to read her mind.

"I just wondered if you'd like to meet up again," he said, almost shyly. "I could show you my collection of estate agent's details," he added, smiling.

"I'd like that. Thanks."

THEY met up the next day, and every day after that. Sometimes they had lunch together, sometimes dinner. Old, well-remembered haunts had been explored.

Mostly, they talked about the past — amusing incidents remembered from long-ago holidays.

Sarah took her camera everywhere and reeled off shots of sunrises and sunsets, birds in hidden lakes, children playing on the moors . . .

She took several photos of Ian, too.

How would she feel, she wondered one day, when she was back home looking at those? The thought was depressing, so she dismissed it.

"It's your last day tomorrow," Ian remarked, as if she needed reminding.

They were walking slowly along the lane at the end of another wonderful day. Sarah had been hoping he would hold her hand . . .

"Yes." She tried to sound bright, happy and cheerful, but she wasn't sure she succeeded.

"Will you be glad to get home?"

"Oh, yes," she lied.

She couldn't bear the thought of going home. Simply couldn't bear it.

"Tell you what," he said, "how about we take a picnic to The Retreat tomorrow night? If we're out for a walk on the moor, we're not trespassing — technically."

"What a good idea!" So good that tears pricked her eyes.

Why was that? Because she was such a sentimental fool that any mention of the old holiday home had that effect on her? Or because it would be her last evening with Ian?

"I'm busy tomorrow," he said, making her spirits sink even lower, "so shall we say about seven?"

"Sounds great!" The forced smile was beginning to make her face ache.

* * * *

Sarah was at The Retreat by six. If there was the slightest chance of Ian arriving even two minutes early — well, she didn't want to miss a single second.

Would they keep in touch once she left? Oh, surely they would. They'd grown so close during this last fortnight that they couldn't simply say goodbye. Could they?

That same question had kept her awake the previous night . . .

"Sarah! Sarah!"

She heard Ian before she saw him, and the urgency in his voice worried her.

But then, when she spotted him racing towards her, he looked so cheerful that she assumed he had good news to tell her.

"I've had a brilliant idea," he announced breathlessly.

Instead of the food he was supposed to bring for their picnic, he was carrying a bulging blue folder. And how could he look so cheerful on their last evening together?

"The Retreat," he said, still breathless as he dropped down on to the sand beside her. "What if we bought it together?"

"What?"

"Yes, listen." He took sheets of paper covered with columns of scribbled figures from the folder. "I've done all the calculations and I think we can do it. If you think of the mortgage on your flat, and add it to the mortgage I'm paying —" His eyes shone with excitement. "We can buy The Retreat between us, Sarah! We could live in it together."

"Live together?" she said in amazement.

"Not live together as in live together." Realising he wasn't making any sense, he explained. "You could have that big bedroom at the back, and I could have the one off the half-landing. We could share the kitchen and bathroom. And the housework, of course.

"That would leave us with two spare bedrooms so I thought that, after we'd done a bit of work on them, we could do bed and breakfast to boost our income."

He stopped, and looked at her.

What did he see in her face? Bewilderment? Certainly that. Disappointment? That, too.

Sarah was speechless. If only he'd said he loved her, loved her as much as she loved him. If only he'd said he couldn't live without her.

"But perhaps you'd rather not," he said flatly.

Now, tears of hurt and disappointment were stinging in her eyes. He had no feelings for her at all. She'd been a fool, to imagine that he had.

"My mistake," he said, crestfallen. "It was a stupid idea."

She began to wonder. Was it such a foolish idea? After all, if they were sharing a house, and a mortgage, perhaps Ian's feelings might develop into something more serious . . .

Funny, though, how little The Retreat meant to her now. It was still her favourite place, of course, but strangely enough, she had just realised it was no longer important to her. It was Ian she loved, not the cottage.

Still, he wasn't to know that.

"I think it's a wonderful idea," she said at last, smiling. "Heavens," she added with a tinkling little laugh, "I'd share a house with Dracula's grandfather if it meant I could live at The Retreat."

"Thanks very much!" But he was laughing.

All thoughts of a picnic forgotten, they sat on the sand and went through all the financial details — right down to the income they could expect from the bed and breakfast venture.

Their hands touched — several times — and at one point, Ian's arm rested lightly on her shoulders.

"Shall we go for it then?" he asked.

"Yes!"

And it was there, sitting on the sand, that he kissed her for the very first time.

THERE were many more kisses after that one, but they never did get around to their bed and breakfast venture. Life seemed to get in the way.

Six months after buying the cottage, they were married. Fourteen months after that, Joshua was born and, eighteen months after that, the twins, Emma and Jayne, arrived . . .

"Thank goodness The Retreat's got four bedrooms," Sarah said as they gazed at the sleeping twins.

"Yes, it's a good job you talked me into buying it," Ian murmured, his arms around her waist.

"I didn't talk you into buying it!"

"Ah, but you did, my love," he murmured. "I would have lived anywhere. For you, it had to be The Retreat. I was frantic, trying to think of some way of keeping you in Exmoor. Suggesting we buy this place was a stroke of genius, don't you think?"

"Pure genius, darling," she agreed with amusement, turning to kiss him.

There was no point telling him now that she would have set up home in a cave so long as it had meant being with him . . . ∎

by Sally Wragg.

Now The Party's Over...

"I WAS going to dig the allotment over this morning, ready for winter," Lennie fretted. He was standing at the window, looking out a little wistfully.

Evelyn frowned. What did he expect at this time of year? Brilliant sunshine?

It was raining, and she was rather stuck for something to do herself. The dishes were washed, the bed made, and she'd already prepared a light salad for lunch.

"Isn't the house quiet?" Lennie observed, his shoulders hunched.

"It's bound to be," Evelyn agreed, folding the tea towel briskly. "All those people . . . wherever did we put them?"

Illustration by Bernie Dowling.

They had just celebrated their golden wedding anniversary. Evelyn still couldn't quite believe how they'd survived it — the months and months of preparation, all the planning, all the invitations to be sent out.

Her sister, Mabel, had come over from Canada — they hadn't seen each other for nine years or more.

Now Mabel had returned to Canada, and Max and Gordon, their sons, had helped them with the clearing up.

The house was spotless, and full of flowers — she'd never seen so many golden flowers out of season. The presents were packed away, the left-over champagne returned to the wholesalers, the extra glass and crockery to the caterers.

That was the problem — after all the pandemonium and uproar and excitement, everything seemed a little bit flat.

"I might slip down to Ben's," Lennie said at last.

Ben was an old chum. The two men tended their allotments together and shared a rickety old tool shed where they brewed tea and put the world to rights.

"Oh, why not?" She sounded a little snippy, and Lennie left without another word.

E VELYN felt annoyed without really knowing why. On impulse, she slipped on her own coat, grabbed her umbrella and went out herself.

A morning's shopping was called for, she thought briskly. It usually managed to cheer her up . . . though she couldn't for the life of her understand why she should need it.

Hadn't she just experienced the most wonderful time of her life? What right had she to feel so sorry for herself?

In town, she peered rather longingly from under her umbrella at one of the dresses in the sales. Now, if only . . .

"Gran! What a surprise to see you here! I thought you and Grandad would still be recovering."

"Hardly!" Evelyn beamed, the dress at once forgotten.

Amy, Gordon's eldest, was her favourite grandchild, and so reminded her of herself. How wonderful to see her! Evelyn felt better already.

"We're not that old, dear — we can stand a little partying!"

"Come and have some tea," Amy insisted. "My treat — you look like you need cheering up. But don't tell me that you and Grandad have had words —" she laughed "— because I simply won't believe you!"

It was a lovely little teashop, all oak beams and an inglenook fireplace with a real wood fire. They found a window seat upstairs, from where they could look down on the high street, busy with multi-coloured umbrellas, and the slanting rain.

It was funny, but it didn't look so bad from this vantage point. And the teashop still served the toasted tea-cakes Evelyn remembered. It was ages since she'd been in; she and Lennie had been far too busy for such things recently.

"I mustn't be too long," Amy chattered on. "I'm going to the pictures later with Tim."

Vaguely, Evelyn remembered a pale-faced boy with long hair.

"Is that who you brought to the party, dear?" She bit into a tea-cake with relish. What a stroke of good fortune to bump into Amy; this was just what she needed.

"That was Ryan . . ." Her granddaughter giggled, delighted at the look on Evelyn's face.

"We're just friends, Gran, that's all. I don't suppose I've actually met anyone yet I really want to get serious over."

She frowned.

"And in any case — how would I know?"

"You'll know, dear," Evelyn said comfortably. "You're young yet."

SHE suddenly realised she hadn't been much older than Amy by the time she had two little boys.

She was rather taken aback at the thought. She poured fresh tea, her mind suddenly full of Lennie, and how things had been.

"Tell me about you and Grandad," Amy urged. "I mean, how did you know he was just the right one?"

"How did I know?" Evelyn mused, stirring her tea, plunged back more years now than she cared to remember.

"It was love at first sight, I suppose. I always knew." She smiled. "I was holidaying in Bath, with my best friend, Nora. Lennie came into the teashop we were in — a teashop just like this one."

No wonder she'd always liked it!

"He was youth-hostelling in the south-west, seeing the sights . . ." She was the best one yet, he'd quipped.

Before he left, he had fixed up a date for the evening. They'd spent an idyllic last two days of their holiday together.

Back home, she and Lennie had written to each other, every day sometimes, and had met up at weekends. They hadn't, after all, lived too far apart. The romance had gathered pace.

Many years had gone by, and now they had celebrated their golden wedding. Where had all that time gone?

"But what was it about him exactly, Gran?" Amy persisted.

"Do you know, love —" Evelyn laughed "– I can't rightly put my finger on it."

She only knew how happy they'd been. She'd never looked at anyone else — never wanted to.

Rather shame-faced, Evelyn thought of how sharp she'd been with him this morning, just because he'd wanted to spend time with an old gardening chum. She was only depressed because the party was over.

She leaned forward and patted Amy's hand.

"Don't worry so — you'll know when you've met someone special. You never know, it may turn out to be this Tim."

"Or Ryan?" Amy teased. "Or there again, there's Jordan — you know, the one I went to the rock festival with the weekend before?"

Evelyn's hand flew to her mouth, but Amy's eyes twinkled merrily. Oh, she was quite cheered up — her granddaughter was incorrigible.

Abruptly, Evelyn thought of Lennie. She was suddenly desperate to get home to him.

But later, as she walked through the front door, shaking the rain from her umbrella, she remembered that Lennie had gone to Ben's. They'd probably be on their third pot of tea by now!

It was a lovely surprise, then, for her to find him at home. The table was set for lunch, and she could hear the kettle coming to boil in the kitchen. What a dear, thoughtful man he was!

It had come to her, walking home in the rain, exactly why she had been feeling so down. And why she'd been so sharp with Lennie.

As if it were his fault!

"You know, Lennie, what with all the partying and everything, we haven't had much time for each other recently," she began.

It was true — it was the one thing that had been lacking in all the wonderful celebrations. Of course, they'd wanted to share their anniversary with family and friends, but hadn't they rather forgotten the most important thing?

"Just what I was thinking, young lady." Lennie's eyes were twinkling now, too. "I've been busy this morning. I didn't get a chance to go down to Ben's. What do you think? I've booked us a weekend away — in Bath!

"We've never been back there, and it'll be the perfect chance to celebrate on our own for once."

How could he have known? It was the perfect place to visit together.

"Do you think we shall find that same little teashop?" he asked. So he hadn't forgotten that, either.

"Oh, Lennie . . ." She frowned momentarily. "But how shall we afford it?" All the celebrations had left such a hole in their budget.

Lennie smiled, the smile she remembered — the smile that always gave her goose-bumps.

"I've been saving for a rainy day," he said smugly. "And it's certainly that, lass!"

The years slipped away, and they might have been the same two young things again. And that was still what they were at heart. ■

ancashire.

This popular centre of holiday entertainment has a population that is swollen every year by the thousands of visitors who flock to its attractions.

The town is packed with all the elements of a vast fun-fair and claims to have everything you could possibly want on a holiday, from old-style tram rides along the sea-front to remedial and sauna baths.

The tower is Blackpool's great landmark, and this engineering feat is always well worth inspecting. From the top of tower you can view the seven-mile-long promenade and take in all the sights of this great holiday resort!

© Pictor International.

Inside Infor

JAKE O'DONNELL was not exactly enthusiastic when his sister phoned to ask him to babysit. There was a disco at the rugby club that evening and he'd been looking forward to it all week.

"Must I?" he asked.

"Yes," Lynne told him firmly.

"You haven't seen the kids in ages, Jake, and they miss you."

"Aw, that's nice," he said, perking up.

"I need you here at six sharp," Lynne went on. "My boss has asked us round for dinner so we can't be late."

"Fair enough," Jake said. There were worse ways to spend a Friday than watching videos and eating crisps with his niece and nephew.

"And you'll have to take the kids to the school Hallowe'en

nation!

by
Alexandra
Blue.

party, too . . ."

Jake panicked.

"Don't tell me I have to dress up!"

"No!" Lynne laughed. "Just drive them there and collect them at eight-thirty."

Jake breathed a sigh of relief. If any of the rugby team were to see him dressed for a children's party, he'd never hear the end of it.

Promising not to be late, he said goodbye and went to pack his overnight bag. He really didn't mind babysitting for

seven-year-old Jordan and five-year-old Katy. They were great kids and he always had a laugh with them.

But the timing was all wrong. He'd planned to sweep Paula Chalmers off her feet at the disco that evening. He'd been dreaming about it all week.

Jake had first spotted Paula about a month ago, when she'd arrived at the club with her brother, who was the team's scrum half.

PAULA was gorgeous. There was no other word for it. And Jake had fallen for her, hook, line and sinker. Not only was she small and slim with blonde curls and blue eyes, but she had the sweetest smile that Jake had ever seen.

But when he'd wangled an introduction, Paula had given him a cool look.

"So you're the famous Jake O'Donnell," she'd said. "I've heard all about you."

Jake was intrigued.

"What have you heard?"

"I know you're good at rugby."

He couldn't deny it.

"I believe you drive a little red sports car."

"I do," Jake confirmed, looking

Illustration by David Young.

111

out of the window at his pride and joy, sitting in the carpark.

"And I've heard you've a different girl for every day of the week."

Jake blinked. It was true he'd had a few girlfriends in his twenty-six years. But he was hardly the Casanova that she was describing.

"I don't know who said that." He'd thrown her brother a dark look. "I'm not that bad!"

"Prove it," Paula said, with a challenging smile.

O VER the next few weeks, Jake did prove he was no ladykiller. He arrived unattached at all the rugby club functions and only had eyes for Paula. But she seemed determined to keep him at arm's length.

"She was badly hurt by her last boyfriend," her brother confided, when Jake asked for some man-to-man advice.

"That's why she left London and came home. She needed the support of her family."

Jake knew all about being badly hurt. His last serious girlfriend, whom he'd been madly in love with, had dumped him when he dared to pause outside a jeweller's shop window.

"Do you think she likes me?" he asked tentatively.

"I reckon so," the scrum half said judiciously. "She's always talking about you. But goodness knows why. You're a right ugly brute."

Jake had laughed at this. He was nicknamed "The Tank" on account of his build, although he reckoned he wasn't bad looking considering the knocks he'd taken on the rugby pitch over the last ten years.

But he didn't think even these imperfections were enough to warrant the cold shoulder treatment. Even when he'd asked Paula to accompany him to the rugby club disco, her reaction had been odd.

"I don't know," she'd said, blue eyes twinkling. "I've heard you're a terrible snorer and that you eat cold beans straight out of a tin. I'm not sure if I want to be associated with a man with such habits."

Jake had been so astonished it took him a few seconds to find his voice.

"Who told you that?"

"I have my sources," she replied, giving him a cheeky grin. "But I'll save you the last dance — if you like."

"I'll keep you to that," Jake said, much heartened.

But his dream of wooing Paula Chalmers had now been scuppered. And it was highly unlikely she would believe he hadn't made the disco because he'd been asked to look after his sister's children. She would probably assume he had been wining and dining one of his numerous lady-friends . . .

When Jake reported for babysitting duties he was met at the door by

Jordan wearing a skeleton outfit.

"Look at you!" Jake exclaimed, giving his nephew a hug. "Excited about the party?"

"You bet!" Jordan said. "But Katy's being a pain."

"Hi, Jake," Lynne said, ushering him into the kitchen. "I'm afraid we have a problem."

Jake began to feel uneasy when she closed the door behind her.

"What's up?"

"One of Katy's friends told her that some of the mums and dads are going to the Hallowe'en party. She wants you to go with her."

"That's OK," Jake said, wondering what all the fuss was about.

Lynne smiled.

"Not so fast. They're all going in fancy dress."

His heart plummeted. If it wasn't bad enough that he was missing the rugby club dance, now he was going to have to dress up and make a fool of himself at a children's party.

"This is stretching the role of a babysitter to the limit, Lynne," he said.

"I know — and I'm sorry. But Jordan is so very excited and if you don't go . . ."

The silence was heavy with emotional blackmail.

"OK, OK," Jake said wearily. "Tell me what I have to wear."

THIRTY minutes later, under the cover of darkness, Jake parked his sports car in the playground. While Jordan scampered on ahead, Jake lifted Katy into his arms and carried her towards the school.

"I love you, Uncle Jake," she said, pressing his nose.

"I love you, too," he muttered, through his teeth.

Kids! Who would have 'em? He would need to keep his fingers crossed that none of the parents were associated with the rugby club. This was so embarrassing.

Sliding into the cloakroom, which was mobbed with small witches, fairies, cowboys, Indians, vampires and ghosts, Jake nodded politely to a harassed mother painting whiskers on to the face of her black cat daughter, and exchanged a sympathetic smile with a father dressed up as Robin Hood.

"I like your tights," Jake said.

The other man looked pained.

"I'm only here under duress."

"Join the club," Jake said feelingly, helping Katy button her silver shoes. She pirouetted and twirled so the shimmery fairy dress fanned out around her.

"Do I look nice, Uncle Jake?"

"You're beautiful," he said indulgently.

Checking to see that there was no-one he knew, he pulled a rubber Dracula mask over his head, adjusted his fangs, slung Lynne's full-length black velvet cape around his shoulders, and gave a maniacal laugh.

"You're silly," Jordan said, rolling his eyes.

"No, he's not," Katy said. She took Jake's hand. "This way."

The school hall was decorated with pumpkin lanterns, skeleton paper chains and fairy lights. The headmaster was trying to organise a ducking for apples competition.

The PTA members were laying dishes of sandwiches, sausage rolls, cheese straws, and cakes decorated with fondant spiders on trestle tables. Music was blasting out of the disco unit.

"Let's dance!" Katy shrieked, jumping up and down.

"Your friends will dance with you, sweetheart," he said, hoping she'd take the hint.

"Wanna dance with you!" Katy yelled, tugging at his cloak.

Grimacing, and almost losing his fangs as a result, Jake allowed himself to be led on to the dance floor and was soon surrounded by a group of girls in their fancy dress costumes. Cinderella's outfit was so huge she kept tripping over the hem and Harry Potter was howling because he'd lost Hedwig.

B UT Jake kept on dancing and allowed his imagination to run riot with images of Paula arriving at the rugby club disco, searching for him in vain, then leaving early, her shoulders slumped with disappointment.

Suddenly, he realised that his dancing partners had all scarpered and he was the only one left.

"Have you been abandoned?" asked someone wearing a black gown and carrying a broom, her face concealed behind a grotesque witch mask.

"Looks like it," he said, adding in a creepy Dracula voice, "do you come here often?"

She laughed.

"All the time, for my sins. I'm a teacher."

Jake was impressed. He reckoned that anybody who could teach this rowdy bunch deserved a medal. Then he saw that Katy was squaring up to a small boy dressed as a WWE wrestler.

"Would you excuse me? My little fairy is in the process of losing her wings."

Katy was furious. The most horrible boy in her class had tried to steal her wings and she was sure they were ripped.

"They're fine," Jake soothed, clipping them back on.

"I'm going to sit with you." She pushed him on to a chair and clambered on to his knee. "It's safer that way."

Parenthood

*T*HE early years of marriage
  Bring problems as we know,
But Kate had found her helpmeet
In the ever-loving Joe.

They welcomed to their family
Two sturdy little boys,
And the birth of Rose, their daughter,
Brought many added joys.

It was a time of sharing
Their children's smiles and tears
And Kate and Joe were happy
In those early married years.

Their healthy brood of children
Grew up, as children do,
And then, as fine young adults
They searched for pastures new.

– Alice Drury.

After the pumpkin lantern competition had been judged, the children were invited to help themselves to party food. Jordan brought Jake a plate filled with tortilla chips and one tiny sandwich.

"Where's my sausage roll?" Jake demanded.

"I didn't think you'd manage to eat it with your fangs," the little boy said seriously.

ROBIN HOOD was consoling a weeping ghost. The children were devouring the party food at an alarming rate. The witch teacher was chatting gaily with the mums from the PTA.

Jake pointed to her.

"Who's that, Jordan?" He wasn't sure why, but there was something about the way she angled her head and moved her hands when she spoke that was familiar to him.

"That's my teacher. She's great and she thinks I'm great, too. Every week we have to write a diary, you know, stuff about our family, what we've been doing. She says my diary is the best she's ever read."

"Clever boy," Jake said, then frowned as the strangest suspicion slid into his mind. "Have you ever mentioned me in your diary?"

"Oh, yes," Jordan said, through a mouthful of crisps. "I've said you play rugby and that you have a sports car. I drew it once."

Jake nodded encouragingly.

"Anything about beans?"

The little boy giggled.

"I said you ate them out of a tin and my mum gave you a row for being lazy."

That was true. Lynne and the family had dropped by his flat one evening and caught him snacking before he went out for rugby training.

"And tell me, Jordan, have you ever written about me having lots of girlfriends?"

Jordan looked coy.

"I just wrote what Mum said, that you've had more girlfriends than she's had hot dinners and she can't see you ever getting married."

"Is that right?" Jake muttered, thinking it was about time he had a little chat with his older sister.

"Have I done something wrong, Uncle Jake?"

Jake looked at his nephew's worried face and shook his head.

"Not at all. In fact, you've just made everything crystal clear. Can I assume that your teacher is called Miss Chalmers?"

"How did you know that?"

"Call it a lucky guess," Jake said, feeling the laughter bubble up inside him as he watched her sweep crisps from the floor with her broomstick. She obviously hadn't seen through his disguise, which gave him the advantage. Yes, it was about time Miss Chalmers had a taste of her own medicine.

As the food was cleared away and the dancing began in earnest, Jake led Paula on to the floor.

"I didn't expect to see you here tonight," Jake said, in a posh, slightly-accented Count Dracula voice. "I heard you'd become a bit of a regular at the rugby club."

She laughed a little nervously.

"News travels fast in a small town."

"And I heard there's someone madly in love with you, but that you've been giving the poor man the runaround."

Paula stared at him.

"Who told you that?"

"Oh, I have my sources," Jake said airily, glad that the vampire mask was concealing his broad grin.

"The poor guy was gutted when he had to babysit his niece and nephew and couldn't make it to the rugby disco."

THERE was a stunned silence. Then her eyes narrowed and she reached up to tug at his mask.

"Jake O'Donnell! I thought you were Jordan and Katy's dad!"

Jake laughed and pulled her into his arms for a slow dance.

"Jordan told me where you got all your information."

She had the good grace to blush.

"You're forgiven," Jake said, pulling her closer when the lights dimmed. He breathed in the clean scent from her hair and gave a contented sigh when she leaned her head against his shoulder.

"Do you believe me now that I don't have loads of girlfriends?"

Her face softened.

"Anybody who dresses like that is no ladykiller."

"Thank you," Jake said. "Are you going on to the rugby club when the party is finished?"

"I did plan to," Paula said, with an impish smile. "But there doesn't seem much point if you won't be there to give me the last dance . . ."

"Why don't we go out tomorrow night instead?" Jake suggested. "Maybe for something to eat?"

Paula looked at him.

"OK," she said finally. "As long as it's not cold beans."

"I think we can come up with something better than that," Jake conceded.

"He likes cold pizza as well," a small skeleton beside them added.

Jake opened his mouth to say something, then decided against it. After all, he had a lot to thank Jordan for, one way and another! ■

Illustration by Peter Gibson.

THE party was lovely. Barbara Collings, newly turned sixty, was enjoying every minute of it.

Her colleagues all sat around her in the wine bar, plying her with drinks.

"Put your money away, love — it's your birthday!" they said.

"Today is the first day of the rest of your life!" Barry, her assistant, added.

She'd worked with them all for so long and had grown really fond of them. They were like the family she'd never had. These young ones, smart little madams with long legs and short skirts, seemed to have no respect for anyone — until you got to know them.

Streetwise and smart-mouthed, underneath it all they were just the same as she had been at their age, loving their mums and little brothers, bringing Barbara their boyfriend problems with touching trust.

"Don't know why you never married, Barbara. You seem to know it all!"

Well, the right person had just never come along. But it had never worried her — she was happy, she had lots of friends and she got on well with her colleagues.

And now she wouldn't see them any more. Today, on her birthday, she was retiring.

A Fresh

Start

by Sylvia Wynne.

"I'll think of you, Barbara, on Monday morning, lying in bed while the rest of us are struggling in to work!" said Dilys, thirty years younger, who was taking over her job.

"Just think, nothing to do all day long — bliss!"

"And a pensioner's pass!" Barry reminded her.

Young Kayleigh giggled.

"You'll be able to ride the buses all day long, Barbara!"

There had been a little ceremony at the office after work before they came here. "Young" Mr Ackroyd, grizzled now and a grandfather, had made a speech thanking her for all her years of faithful service — why, she remembered "old" Mr Ackroyd, his father!

Everyone clapped, and Barry had made the presentation of a microwave oven.

Thanking them with tears glistening in her eyes, she'd wondered ruefully whether she'd ever use it, with all day long in which to prepare her simple meals. There would be no coming in tired and wanting something quick.

No watching the clock now. Funny that people used to be presented with a clock on retirement, when time had ceased to matter. It seemed the microwave was the modern equivalent.

"You're all so kind!" she said now, pressing Kayleigh's hand, clutching Barry's arm, smiling tearfully at Dilys, and Di, who she often had lunch with and who told her all her marital troubles.

Correction — had told her. Despite promises to keep in touch, Barbara doubted if they'd ever meet regularly again.

THEN it was over. People began to slip away; there were hugs, kisses, good wishes, even a few tears.

Finally, Colin Lomax, one of the reps, came over.

"I'll drive you home, Barbara," he said. "I live in your area. That microwave's a bit awkward to take on the Tube."

She was grateful, as she'd been wondering how she'd manage. She got into his firm's car, reflecting that in all her years of service she'd never learned to drive.

"I really envy you, Barbara," Colin said, carrying the microwave into her spotless kitchen with its plants and bright pots and crockery, and thumping it down on to the work surface.

"Retirement!" He sighed. "It won't be till sixty-five for me. The kids reared, the mortgage paid, just the wife and me to take off on our own. We could sail round the world."

"Sail round the world?" Barbara gasped. She'd always thought of him as the conventional family man, beer-with-the-lads-at-weekends type. "Won't you be a bit old?"

"Sixty-five's not old!" Colin laughed. He held out his hand and shook hers warmly.

"All the best now, love, and see you enjoy yourself!"

"Well, thanks," Barbara stammered, feeling tongue-tied all over again. "And for the lift."

How kind people were! She hadn't realised until now, when it was a bit late.

She made herself a cup of tea and drank it sitting in the kitchen. She stared dismally at the microwave in the ruins of its festive wrappings, surmounted by a huge card which had been signed by them all. Oh, how she was going to miss them!

She was so tired. She'd been working all out for the last few weeks, getting everything in order for Dilys, her successor. And she'd never felt more lonely in her life, not even when her parents died.

THE weekend dragged. All the things she normally did, like getting in the shopping, changing the bed and putting on a wash, sorting out her clothes for Monday, seemed pointless when now she'd have all week to do them.

On Sunday night she went to bed early, dreading the morning.

She slept well. She awoke at her usual time, seven o'clock, but of course, the alarm didn't go off.

She lay there for a minute. Goodness, Dilys was right, Barbara thought. She's struggling out of bed to start her Monday battle, but I can turn over and go back to sleep!

So she did. An hour later, she stumbled out of bed, pulled on her dressing-gown, and went downstairs and out into the back garden.

It was a beautiful morning, mid-September, a touch of autumn in the air, the sun just dispersing the mist. Dew sparkled on the grass, and diamond-chains of cobwebs glittered in its low rays.

Barbara sat down carefully on the damp garden seat. She'd never been out in the garden in her dressing-gown before, but, well, who was there to see?

Her neighbours were all struggling, like Dilys, with their early morning routine, stumbling sleepily out of the house into buses and on to the Tube. She alone was privileged to sit here in the strengthening sunshine, listening to the chirping of the birds and marvelling at the dewdrops on every leaf.

She was amazed at the sheer beauty of an ordinary suburban morning, which she'd never before had the time to appreciate.

And she could do whatever she liked! She could sit here for an hour if she wanted to, until hunger drove her indoors. She could make a cup of tea and drink it at her leisure, reading her post and the newspaper, deciding how to spend her day.

For years, she reflected, she'd wanted to learn a language, but had never seemed to get up the energy. Well, now she could.

She could get out her bus pass, like Kayleigh had said. She could go to a museum, an art gallery — the shops even, though she'd have to watch the pennies a bit more now. Or she could decorate the house, room by room, take her time over it . . .

She didn't want to sail round the world like Colin — though if sixty-five wasn't old, sixty certainly wasn't — but there were friends she could go and see.

Norah, her old school-friend, had been begging her to come for a visit for years — and why not, with her senior citizen's railcard? It would be nice to see Norah again.

SUDDENLY, a world of incredible possibilities opened up before Barbara's eyes. What an old misery she'd been — and a bit of a coward as well — stuck in her groove, always tired! Why had she not seen that?

But now, after a weekend of idleness with the pressure off, she felt herself springing back to life like flattened grass.

She'd miss the office, of course, and her friends there, but she'd make other friends. The world was full of potential company; she just had to seek it out.

"See you enjoy yourself!" Colin Lomax had said. And what were Barry's words?

"Today is the first day of the rest of your life."

How right he was! And it was going to start right this minute!

She went into the house to make a cup of tea and have breakfast, already planning her day.

She might even just spend it in the garden. ∎

Lanhydrock, Cornwall

THINK of clotted cream, pasties and cider, think of Cornwall. But there's more to this gorgeous county than mere food and drink!

It's a treasure trove of leafy lanes, beautiful gardens, picturesque shorelines and brooding moorland.

Don't forget to visit the wonderful Lost Gardens Of Heligan, where the moist conditions and mild temperatures experienced in Cornwall allow sub-tropical species of plants to thrive.

Illustration by Gerard Fay.

All You Nea

IT was strange, but when my daughter Emily left home for the first time to go to art college in London, I seemed to miss the noise and mess left by her friends more than I did her.

I used to love having them stay over after a party. One night there had been seven girls in all, and we'd had to have a rota for the bathroom!

I had been the one who'd encouraged Emily to go to college, but London was a long

way from Devon and I wasn't that confident about driving these days.

It wasn't that I couldn't drive, I'd just got out of practice and had lost some of my confidence. I could nip round our village and to the supermarket and back in my little car, but negotiating motorways and busy city centres felt beyond me.

Ever since my husband, Jeff, had died, I had just had to get on with it, but I still didn't like

124

dealing with roundabouts and busy junctions.

Emily, of course, took them in her stride. She was a good driver, just like her father had been, and I had been very tempted to let her take my little car with her when she went.

Emily, however, had decided against that herself.

"No, parking near the flat is just impossible, Mum. Anyway, you need it for the shopping and stuff. And you'll need it to visit me, won't you? You'll just have to learn to deal with roundabouts . . ."

She knew I had a particular hatred of roundabouts. Well, they don't have any in our village, and I just wasn't sure what to do on one. I tried to explain this to Emily.

a toddler, I had travelled round the countryside giving cookery demonstrations. I wasn't in the league of all these modern culinary experts, but my late husband, Jeff, had always praised my "good, honest British food" and the paying guests we'd taken in on the farm had never seemed to complain.

WITH Emily gone, I decided I would take this up again and went to the local adult education centre to brush up on modern methods. There are still a lot of Women's Clubs who like demonstrations where they can watch and ask questions, and taste the finished product!

Is Love by Judy Chard.

"You just have to follow the arrow that points in the direction of the place you want. It's all painted on the road . . ."

"But that's just it. I always seem to be on top of the signs before I can actually read them!"

She took me in her arms and hugged me.

"Don't worry, Mum. I'll be back as often as I can and I'll give you some refresher driving lessons then."

Years ago, when Emily had been

I got all my ingredients locally, of course. The meat came from Pete's butcher's shop. He had been a lifelong friend of Jeff's; they had gone to school together.

Pete had never married, but it hadn't seemed to matter, and over the years he became just like part of the family. Jeff had once teased him about having no wife, and Pete had looked away and muttered something about "not being very good at commitment".

Later, when we were alone,

Jeff had turned to me.

"I think Pete fancies you, Marian. He's got my good taste!"

He'd kissed the end of my nose and, for some silly reason, I'd blushed. Nothing could have been further from my mind, because much as I liked Pete, there had never been, and never could be, anyone for me but Jeff.

However, now that I was on my own, Pete had become a tower of strength. He spent a lot of time helping me with the financial side of things. When Jeff died I had sold the land that went with the farm and kept the house, although it was really too big now Emily was at college.

I told myself that I was staying there so that she could come home and visit, and not because I just couldn't bear to leave my memories behind. I'm not sure who was kidding who, but after a few weeks Emily came home for the weekend.

THINKING back, I suppose my phone calls had been rather full of Pete and how helpful he was, but I never dreamed she'd react the way she did when I asked her to lay an extra place for Sunday lunch.

She looked up for a moment, then rattled the cutlery drawer meaningfully.

"I like Uncle Pete, Mum, but he could never take Dad's place, could he?"

I was taken aback for a moment. I suppose I had never really thought about Pete that way.

"He's always been part of our family, Emily, you know that."

She shrugged her shoulders, but there was a definite chill in the air when Pete came over. I could tell that he was puzzled by it.

I realised Emily was not the schoolgirl I'd waved goodbye to some weeks before. She was still my lovely daughter, of course, but she seemed much more sophisticated, had lots more confidence in herself.

In her absence, Pete had got used to popping in when he felt like it and I had given him a key. He had suggested it, just in case I had an accident or locked myself out or something.

Emily wasn't happy about this.

"Mum, is it wise to let Pete have a key? He might wander in when you're in the shower or anything . . ."

I explained what Pete had said about having an accident and she almost exploded.

"Good grief! Anyone would think you needed a Zimmer frame!"

I tried to laugh it off but I realised that she was serious.

The rest of the weekend passed pleasantly enough, but without quite the happy atmosphere I had hoped for. She wasn't actually rude but she did vanish very soon after Pete arrived, and hardly joined in our conversations. I had to admit it was quite a relief when it was time for her to leave.

PETE came to supper after she had gone and I could see he had something on his mind. Usually he ate with enjoyment, but tonight he was just playing with his steak.

"What's the matter, Pete? Don't tell me your steak is tough? It's one of yours, you know!" I tried to keep the situation light, but he put his knife and fork down with a sigh.

"The food is wonderful as always, Marian. That's not what's wrong — it's Emily, and her attitude towards you. It's as if no-one else has a right to your company and she wants you all to herself."

"That's ridiculous!" I leapt to her defence automatically.

"She's changed since she's been away, Marian. She acts like I'm an outsider. I think she's had you to herself for too long since Jeff died. She's probably thinking I'm trying to take his place, get my feet under the table or something."

"Don't say that, Pete. I'm sure you're wrong. She adored her father, that's all. She's hurt and I suppose I should have confided in her more. I gave her all my love and tried to make up for a father's love as well."

"There is a limit to how much of yourself you can give, Marian," he said slowly.

It was the closest Pete and I had ever been to a row. I felt really upset when he left. After that we still saw each other, but something had gone out of the old, casual, warm friendship.

To keep myself busy, I resolved to carry on with my cookery demonstrations, and luckily the education people put me on their list. Secretly, I was relieved, as I could make genuine excuses for not seeing Pete as much.

✳ ✳ ✳ ✳

Just before Christmas I had a letter from an old school friend who lived in Cornwall, suggesting Emily and I stay with her for the holiday. I was really grateful as I hadn't been looking forward to the festive season.

Kathy had been a great support when Jeff died, so I rang Emily and, to my surprise, she jumped at the idea. I suppose she was relieved she wouldn't have to be civil to Pete over the holidays.

Emily insisted I drive to Kathy's and, with her sitting beside me, I had to admit that the roundabouts did lose some of their menace.

The weather was wonderful, the days almost as warm as summer with clear blue skies, and a glittering frost at night.

Kathy had three sons; the youngest, Ian, was about the same age as Emily. They seemed to hit it off at once.

I hardly saw her as he took her riding over the moors, played bowls at the local pub and even started to teach her golf. In the evenings they all went "clubbing", and Emily came back with a real sparkle in her eyes.

We were both sorry when the week came to an end, and Emily seemed more like her old self as she chatted happily about the time she and Ian had spent together.

"He's going to be a mining engineer, did you know? He went backpacking in Oz last year and joined an archaeology dig." Her face lit up with a kind of inner glow as she

talked — and I realised my daughter was falling in love.

The only downside to the week had been my guilt at leaving Pete to spend Christmas alone. Our relationship had almost returned to its former warmth in Emily's absence, and I realised now how much I missed him when we were apart.

THE weeks flew by and Easter was on the horizon. I was giving some special demonstrations of cakes and Easter eggs for my cookery classes. With so much driving, I had become quite skilled and could now even cope with roundabouts!

I was wondering if I should ask Pete to lunch on Easter Sunday, but hesitated because I didn't want to upset Emily.

She, however, didn't seem to be that bothered about Pete. She said she was hoping to see Ian after Easter as he was probably moving to London for a little while before he went to Australia — it was pretty obvious the phones had been busy all round.

But as soon as she got off the train a few days later I could see

Buteshire

Lochranza stands at the head of a sea-inlet at the tip of the island of Arran, and is a favourite with island visitors and holidaymakers alike.

A lovely ferry ride takes you to Lochranza which is popular all year round with tourists. There are many outdoor pursuits here, and beautiful gardens that are well worth a visit.

Don't forget to seek out the 14th century half-ruined castle, either. It's famous for being one of the places on Arran in which Robert the Bruce stayed on his return to Scotland at the beginning of his campaign.

Spectrum Colour Library.

something was wrong.

She did manage a smile and a hug, and said it was lovely to see me, but that was all. I couldn't help wondering if something had gone wrong between her and Ian. First love always was painful, but she didn't know that, did she?

She spent the few days before the Easter weekend reading magazines, the mobile phone never far from her hand. Sometimes she sat in her room, playing light classical music, something I had never heard her do before.

I remembered then she had once said Ian loved some of the more popular classics. I almost wished we could have the monotonous beat of her usual pop music back.

On Easter Saturday she disappeared soon after breakfast.

"Shan't be long," she said, as she pulled on her walking shoes.

She wasn't gone long, and at breakfast on Easter morning she seemed much more like her old self. In fact, there was a secret smile on her face, as if she knew something I didn't. She kept glancing at her watch, too.

Could it be she had heard from Ian, and that he was going to ring? I didn't dare ask in case I upset her. She certainly never mentioned him — it was almost as if Christmas had never happened.

As we washed the breakfast things she finally told me what had happened.

"I rang Ian at the end of term as I hadn't heard from him for a bit. He isn't coming up to London after all, he's going straight to Australia.

There's the chance of some kind of sabbatical for a year."

She stopped for a moment, her voice thick with emotion. I refrained from making any comment; it would be an intrusion, and I had to hear more.

"I could tell from his voice that our whole time together hadn't really meant anything special to him — not like it had to me. He didn't even suggest we keep in touch by e-mail or anything . . . there was nothing." She paused again.

"I'll never love anyone else again like I loved him. I know it was only a short time, but I thought it was the same for him. I didn't know what love meant when I heard people talk about it — that longing to belong, be the other half of someone. Now I do know and it's awful . . ."

S UDDENLY she was in my arms — her heart broken, a feeling I knew only too well, none the less painful because she was young. I thought of all the useless words and clichés about time healing everything, about growing up — and buried them.

"At least I'm grown up now and not an ignorant, spiteful kid. I'm sorry, Mum, I've been a selfish brat."

Again there was that quick smile and secret look. I was about to reply when the doorbell rang.

"Oh, hang on a minute. I'll just see who that is."

It was Pete who stood on the doorstep, a big square envelope in his hand. He held it out to me.

"I had personal instructions yesterday from the sender. I was told to deliver it this morning."

I glanced round quickly to see if Emily had followed me but she had gone upstairs, and I could hear one of her favourite pop songs playing again.

I opened the envelope with shaking fingers. Inside was a beautiful hand-painted card of spring flowers, and written underneath in Emily's round handwriting were the words, *The bearer of this card is sent as my personal Easter present to you, darling Mum.*

So that was what that smile had meant! Suddenly it all made sense.

Pete grinned at me.

"It's quite flattering, being someone's Easter present. I couldn't be happier." And he drew me into his arms, and we smiled because at that moment the sound of Easter bells from the church filled the air.

I knew that things wouldn't be all plain sailing from here on in, but Pete and I had each other. And, one day, Emily would meet a special someone, too, and then we could all celebrate this very special time of year together. ∎

Rose's Wedding

*H*OW *quickly time goes by, and now*
Their children were full-grown.
Both their sons had married
And had children of their own.

And Rose, their only daughter
Now planned to marry, too,
And said she'd have her wedding
Before the year was through.

And on that special wedding day
Joe felt a swell of pride
As, walking slowly down the aisle,
He led the lovely bride.

And Kate was moved to shed a tear
As Rose became a wife,
And proudly and with dignity
Embarked on her new life.

– Alice Drury.

Illustration by Mark Viney.

by Silvie Taylor.

I T was Thursday and the restaurant was crowded. He'd known it would be; he was banking on it. It meant he could sit there in his corner, observing but unobserved, pencil poised, pretending to study the crossword.

He looked at his watch. Ten minutes past six. Maybe she wouldn't come. On the other hand, being late, where Sally was concerned, was par for the course.

In the old days, when their marriage was new and full of hope, she'd meet him here every Thursday after work and they'd spend for ever deciding what to order, a limited budget the deciding factor.

Later, when promotion for both had eased the purse strings, they'd

132

Swan Song

moved upmarket for this weekly treat, to Ricardo's at first and, very occasionally, to Parsifal's on the outskirts of town, all silver service and starched napkins, with a view of larches dipping frail fronds in a loch where swans drifted, slow, smooth, elegant.

Anton was their favourite waiter, he remembered. If things were quiet he'd pick up one of the stiff damask squares and fashion it swiftly into a swan.

"Again, Anton, and slowly this time," Sally had commanded, and so he'd shown her again, nodding in approval as she mastered the art in one.

That was Sally — quick of eye, deft of hand and always smiling. In those days, at least.

Idly, he toyed with the flimsy paper napkin tucked into the glass in front of him. She'd have dismissed it as a mere serviette. It was blue. Who'd ever heard of a blue swan?

Pushing his unused

cutlery aside, he smoothed the paper on the bare formica and made the first fold, trying to remember.

He'd always been the more sentimental of the two, urging his wife to return here each year on his birthday.

"Say yes, Sal? Just to please me."

And she'd agree, but with increasing reluctance year by year.

S ALLY had taken to prosperity with an alacrity which surprised him. She'd enjoyed playing the perfect hostess in their elegant home, shopping in the most expensive designer stores. He'd smiled indulgently. Things would be different when the longed-for family arrived.

Tentatively, he folded the corners then pressed them down firmly.

From campsites in France they'd moved on to holidays in Tenerife, an occasional cruise — there really was no place like the Caribbean, Sally said — until, finally, they had their own villa in the Algarve.

"Let's do it," she'd said. "It'll be fun, you'll see. You know how much you miss your golfing cronies when they're out there. And I miss the girls. Think of the sunshine. No more looking anxiously at the sky, wondering if you'll reach the nineteenth before the downpour."

Very persuasive, Sally; and, yes, it had been fun. True, it hadn't always been easy, watching their friends' youngsters splashing around in the pool and squealing with joy.

They'd given up hope of a family of their own by that time.

He'd been proud of her, the way she'd hidden a heavy heart beneath that bright smile. It became more brittle as sophistication took over. Sometimes he hardly recognised the breathless, naive teenager he'd married, but he was always proud of her.

Another fold, another crease. Was that how Anton had created the wings? Was this the corner he'd tweaked out with a flourish and, hey presto, a beak?

No, he'd got it wrong — terribly wrong. As he had so many things. He'd provided the lifestyle to which his wife had become addicted, but it

134

hadn't been enough.

When she couldn't remould him to her idea of the perfect husband, she'd simply said, "It's no good, Michael."

She'd even stopped calling him Mike.

"We're not right for one another any more. Time to call it a day. Shall I move out, or will you?"

Sudden, just like that. Typical of Sal. Quick, decisive.

The napkin was limp now with folding and refolding. Hands damp with perspiration didn't help. Why wouldn't the wings flap the way they were supposed to? He'd forgotten how.

He hadn't been able to forget Sally so easily, but then he hadn't wanted to, if the truth were known.

"There's no-one else," she'd assured him, and there hadn't been, to begin with.

He'd followed her progress through the local press, where her photograph appeared most weeks, showing her poised, sleek and tailored to perfection, as befitted a company director. The Sally he'd known was curly-headed and bubbly, nice to know and nicer still to love.

It had been a year or two before she'd married the managing director, a balding little man who lived life in the fast lane, which was exactly where he was when his black sports car (Sally's was red) slewed off a sharp bend and into a tree.

S O there she was, his only love, married, divorced, remarried and now a widow. Was she the same, he wondered, under that glossy sophistication? Probably not. After all, he'd changed, too.

It was strange that they'd seldom bumped into each other over the years, living in the same town, knowing the same people.

It was facing this special birthday that had prompted him to get in touch at last. Not by telephone, though. After some deliberation he'd sent a note, telling himself that only curiosity prompted it.

Come and wish me Happy Birthday, he'd written. *Same time, usual place.*

He hesitated before signing, then, defiantly, wrote *Mike* in a firm hand.

It had probably gone straight into her stainless steel waste bin. Oh, well. Another five minutes, no more.

The waitress hovered, refilled his coffee cup and, though he was unaware of it, having given up on the swan and turned back to his crossword, gave him a sympathetic look.

She shook her head as she returned to where her colleague was making out someone's bill.

"Poor chap. Been sitting there nearly an hour. Said when he arrived he'd be ordering for two. Some women don't know when they're lucky.

He's really quite a dish."

Another few minutes passed. He'd started on the swan again, with the napkin that should have been Sally's. This time, when he pulled the tail feathers the wings did move, but in the wrong direction.

He crumpled it up in disgust. Just like me and Sal, he thought, always travelling in opposite directions.

No point in looking at the menu. It hadn't changed in years, and in any case he was no longer hungry. She wasn't coming. It had been a stupid whim on his part. He should have known better.

Here was the waitress again. No, he wouldn't have any more coffee, thanks.

"Just the bill. Looks as though my friend couldn't make . . ."

BUT what was this she was holding out to him? A paper swan, pristine white and perfectly fashioned.

"I'm sorry, sir. We were meant to give you this when you came in, but we didn't see it until a few minutes ago. Tracy, that's the afternoon girl, left a note saying a lady handed it in."

"For me? How did you know it was for me?"

"'For a gentleman who'll arrive spot on six and probably be wearing a blazer.' I'm really sorry we didn't see it sooner."

"No harm done."

She hesitated as he continued to examine the swan.

"No note?"

"Just the one Tracy left for us, sir."

"No problem. Just my bill then, when you've a minute."

He laid the bird in front of him, admiring its sharp precision. Then, sure of the result, he tested the wings. The movement was faultless.

He knew exactly what to do next. Quickly, he unfolded each sharp crease, not bothering to analyse how it had been put together, but eager to read what she'd written.

Happy Birthday, Michael! Not Mike. It still rankled. *What's the point in slumming? Will be at Parsifal's from seven.*

No, Sally hadn't changed. Everything had to be done her way — even on his birthday.

He left the swan behind him, a little heap of white snowflakes, paid his bill and rewarded the bemused waitress with a smile and generous tip, then strode out into the evening sunshine, a tall, upright figure with a spring in his step.

Hailing a taxi, he smiled to himself as they passed the road to Parsifal's and headed instead for his club.

No, Sally would never change.

And on his seventieth birthday, it was finally time to move on. ∎

S HE'D take all this stuff to the People's Dispensary for Sick Animals, Laura thought suddenly. That's what she would do.

by Valerie Edwards.

A Family Tradition

Mum had always supported them. Whenever she had had a clear-out, she used to take her old books and clothes and whatever there.

She'd always said the PDSA must have been a Godsend to people who couldn't afford vets' fees. But that had been Mum all over — always willing to help someone else out.

Laura stood up and rubbed her back. She'd sifted through everything, determined to finish the job and make neat piles.

Mum would have been proud; she'd berated Laura for her untidiness often enough in the past.

"Like chalk and cheese, we are." She'd sighed. "Mind you, wouldn't do if we were all the same, would it? I bet I drive you mad, too, sometimes, girl."

Girl . . . Laura remembered, with a pang, that she'd always been "girl" to Mum. She'd liked it. It had made her feel special, somehow.

She put out a hand and smoothed the dark red blouse on top of the nearest stack. It was almost new and she'd admired it no end when Mum had carried it home in triumph from their local department store's spring sale.

Now, she would have kept it and worn it herself, but Mum had been so petite that she'd had to buy a special size. Not only that, but Mum had never seemed to put any weight on, while Laura had gradually crept up in size over the years. That was another way in which they were so different.

Laura's own daughter, Jill, was like Mum, though. Small, neat, and dainty in appearance and in habits!

Laura smiled. She had always liked to look at Jill and point out her resemblance to Mum. And Mum had been as proud as punch to think her pretty granddaughter took so much after her.

She stepped back and jumped at the sudden yelp.

"Oh, Jack," she said anxiously. "I'm so sorry. Are you all right?"

She bent and gathered the little Westie into her arms.

"You must be feeling neglected enough without me stepping on you, you poor thing."

Jack licked her hand with a small pink tongue.

"You miss her as much as I do, don't you?" Laura set the dog down gently on the carpet again and her eyes filled with tears as he slumped against her feet. She took a deep breath.

"Now, come on, Jack, we can't have that. She'd have told us smartly to buck our ideas up, wouldn't she? And so we shall. Even if it is Saturday."

I SHALL go into town and have coffee and a doughnut at the Mirabel, just as Mum and I always used to, she thought. It was always our special day out.

She sighed to herself, remembering. Years and years ago, just occasionally — when she'd been busy or there had been something else on — she'd seen it as a bit of a chore.

Having said that, she'd never missed a Saturday they'd arranged, not once. Nor had Mum. It was special to both of them.

After their coffee and a natter they'd go round the shops, gazing in the expensive boutique windows and then searching for bargains elsewhere.

One of them would sit on a chair, carefully sizing up the top or skirt the other was thinking of buying. Then they'd come to a joint decision and either buy the garment or not. Then they'd go off to the library to change their books.

"And in the afternoon, Jack," Laura said to the little dog, "we'd go down to the quay and get the ferry across the canal to the little café on the other side, for sandwiches and lovely strawberry ice cream."

Then it'd be time to go and collect Jill from her friend's house. A perfect Saturday!

"Look at the time," Laura said aloud. "Come on, Jack, time to move."

She settled the dog in his basket with his favourite biscuit and picked up the first pile of clothes. The little car seemed to groan as she filled the boot and then started on the back seat, and she gave it a comforting pat as she trudged off for the final load.

Mum had always done that, she remembered suddenly — every single time they'd reached the end of a journey in it.

"It doesn't hurt to say thanks for getting us here safely," she'd say if Laura caught her in the act. And Laura would shake her head and roll her eyes, but they'd both know she didn't mean it.

Laura gave Jack a final stroke and then went out, locking the door behind her.

THE charity shop were very pleased to see her. Her mother had been such a regular visitor — Laura often accompanying her — that all three assistants came out to help bring the bags in.

"We'll miss your mum," the small pony-tailed one said. "She had us in stitches sometimes with her wicked sense of humour. And thanks so much for thinking of us and bringing all this stuff in."

Laura nodded, too choked to say anything. She got back in her car and sat there for a moment, staring through the windscreen.

An impatient motorist trying to park hooted behind her and she started and gathered herself before she drew away.

Now, although she was having second thoughts, she made herself turn right at the roundabout and head towards the Mirabel. Finding that she'd got the last space in the café's small carpark cheered her up a bit.

Her sudden cheer was soon dispelled, however, when through the window, she spotted someone else already sitting at their favourite table.

In fact, the café was so crowded she couldn't see a vacant seat anywhere. Biting her lip, she pushed open the door anyway.

And paused.

And in that instant, the person sitting at the table turned and looked straight at her. A huge smile swept over the girl's face.

Jill! It was Jill! How had she guessed that her mother would turn up? It was marvellous!

Laura was breathless by the time she reached her. She sat down in the chair her daughter pulled out for her, lost for words.

"I couldn't let the family ties die, Mum," Jill said with a smile. "I mean, you and Gran. And now me and you.

"And perhaps in time, a long time from now, it'll be Debbie and me. It's sort of special, isn't it?"

"Oh, Jill," Laura said faintly. "It's so nice to hear you say that. I've been thinking about Gran all morning and she would have loved this."

"Gran would have been pleased, wouldn't she? 'Good on you both!' I can just hear her saying it. Can't you?"

"Yes, I can. Your gran would have been delighted." Laura smiled. She was beginning to feel very happy now. Very happy indeed.

"Paul's going to take Debbie to the football every Saturday — you know what a little tomboy she is!" Jill began to giggle. "And I'm going to start doing the supermarket shop on a Tuesday night after work.

"Not only will it leave Saturday free for my special day out with you, but it'll be quieter and a lot less hassle without Debbie in tow!"

Jill leaned over and patted her mum's hand tenderly.

"Now, are you ready for coffee and doughnuts? I know I am — I've been looking forward to it all morning!" ∎

Seil Island, Argyll

ONE of the Inner Hebrides, the island of Seil to the south of Oban lies so close to the mainland that it's connected to it by a bridge.

Designed by Telford in 1792, it's known as the Atlantic Bridge, because it's the only structure of its kind to cross Atlantic water.

Seil has an attractive village of whitewashed cottages, roofed with slate from the neighbouring small and much-quarried island of Easdale. Slate was the main industry on Seil, too, and you'll see evidence of it everywhere you go on this beautiful island.

SEIL ISLAND, ARGYLL: J CAMPBELL KERR.

ARE you all right, love?" Barney put the coffee cups down on the side table and smiled hopefully at his wife, rather alarmed by the dark smudges of tiredness he saw under her eyes.

In the cot by the window, the baby stirred. She was a fretful child. Alysha only hoped she wasn't going to start crying again. She had never imagined that life with a new baby could be so wearing.

"I was just trying to think of a name," she said.

"Again?" he teased. "Oh, any old name will do. What about Thingy? At least we'll be original."

"Oh, Barney!"

Too late, he realised she wasn't in the mood for jokes.

"I really don't mind," he assured her. "Whatever you want is just fine."

"But it's got to be something that we both want," she insisted stubbornly.

They hadn't even registered the birth yet. What was the matter with them? They just couldn't seem to hit upon a name that suited them both.

What's In A Name?

by Susie Riggott.

And naming a first baby was special, whatever Barney was trying to say to the contrary.

"There must be a compromise," Alysha said quietly. She looked so anxious.

Barney was worried about her — about them both. Who would have believed a tiny baby could so consume every waking hour?

THE child was making tiny mewling noises now, like a kitten. Revving herself up to full cry, Alysha supposed. Unfortunately, being so new to the job, she hadn't yet worked out quite what to do about such minor emergencies. The baby wasn't due a feed. She'd already changed her. Now what was she supposed to do?

Illustration by Steve Caldwell.

The baby's eyes were open. She had extraordinarily wise eyes, staring intently at her mother, as if she might have had quite a lot to say in this difficult naming business, if only they had the commonsense to ask her.

"She doesn't look like she wants to sleep," Barney remarked, peering over Alysha's shoulder. "Should we take her for a walk? The fresh air might do the trick."

"I suppose so." Alysha frowned. "Perhaps we could try to think of a name whilst we're about it."

143

The day was surprisingly warm. The sky was clear, the sun high. Obligingly, the baby snuggled into her pram and closed her eyes. Was she sleeping? They hardly dared to hope.

"I wish I wasn't so tired," Alysha grumbled.

"But is it any wonder?" Barney himself was yawning, though he did his best to stifle it. "We're lucky if we can get a couple of hours together."

"I wish . . ." she began, and faltered.

"What do you wish?"

They were walking across the green, past the village bonfire. It was the fifth of November — how could they have forgotten the party that night?

He turned towards her.

"Tell me what you wish."

What did she wish? That she had a mother of her own? Someone else to turn to? Alysha's mum had died shortly after she was born. Her dad had done his best, bless him, but sometimes . . .

"I wish I didn't feel so uncertain about things," she said.

W HAT was the matter with her? Didn't she have everything she'd ever wanted? A lovely husband, a beautiful baby?

Her face fell.

"I can't even think of a simple name . . ."

"We can't," Barney corrected her, and then he smiled gently, wanting more than anything to cheer her up.

He nodded towards the crazy-looking figure perched on top of the collection of wood, branches, old furniture and odds and ends from sheds and outhouses. The whole village had pitched in. This was going to be the bonfire to end all bonfires.

"What a shame she's not a boy. We could have called her Guy!"

"I think I'll give the bonfire party a miss tonight, Barney." She yawned. It was too soon; she didn't feel ready to go out and about.

"But Mum says she'll babysit — if we don't mind taking Aiden." Aiden was Barney's youngest brother.

The Hardys were a large, noisy family — how Alysha envied them! She and Barney had always talked of having a large, noisy family of their own. Now she wasn't so sure.

"I can see it all from the bedroom window," she said.

And though she liked Barney's mum a lot, she was just a tiny bit in awe of her. Alysha didn't know how she had managed over the years with such a large family — not to mention all the charity work she did, helping out at Aiden's school, her hectic social life . . . How did she fit it all in?

Meanwhile, Alysha's world had been turned upside down by the arrival of this one tiny scrap of humanity.

"Are you quite sure, love?" Barney asked later, getting ready to go out.

He hated to leave her.

"You have a good time," she insisted. "I'll be all right here. I can see as much of it as I want."

So long as she could keep her eyes open. She watched him from the bedroom window. Over on the green, someone had lit the bonfire. Already, bright tongues of flame wrapped around its massive shape.

The baby stirred in her cot. The night was a sharp one, the sky ink-black. There would be a frost in the morning.

Rockets exploded like giant stars fizzing across the firmament. On the green, a huge roman candle sparked, sending up an irridescent shower of reds and greens.

A LYSHA — are you there?" a voice called from downstairs. Wearily, Alysha went down to meet Barney's mum. Just what she didn't need.

"I was wondering if you might have changed your mind about the bonfire," the older woman said. "But you look all in, love! Is there anything I can do?"

"Not really." Alysha smiled. "I'm just a bit tired," she said, to soften her refusal.

Elizabeth took off her coat and sat down on the sofa beside her.

"I can remember when I brought our Susie home," she said, the beginnings of a smile hovering. Susie was her eldest, Barney's big sister. "We never slept a wink."

Alysha perked up.

"But you've always seemed so . . . well, capable and efficient."

Elizabeth laughed.

"Then it only goes to show how deceptive looks can be! When the poor little thing actually did sleep, I generally managed to wake her again, checking everything was still in working order. Poor baby! How did she survive us?"

She looked at Alysha's tired face. She'd been meaning to have this talk with her, but hadn't known quite how to start it. And she'd been a little afraid of sticking her nose in, she supposed. But she knew exactly what Alysha was going through — hadn't she been through it herself?

Poor lass, she looked washed out. Elizabeth was glad she'd taken the time to come across. She leaned forward and tapped Alysha's knee gently.

"Shall I put the kettle on?"

When her mother-in-law left a good hour later, it was amazing how much better Alysha felt. Talking had done her so much good. And she felt reassured that she wasn't useless, or a hopeless novice as a mother.

Elizabeth had said all new mothers felt the same, though Alysha would never have believed it. With a start, she realised suddenly the baby was quiet — too quiet?

She flew upstairs, only to discover her sleeping peacefully. She laughed a little nervously, relief flooding through her. Peering into the cot at her daughter's downy head, she found herself overwhelmed again by the same tidal wave of love.

Elizabeth said it was all perfectly normal, that things, somehow, would fall into place. They were both getting to know each other, that was all.

Alysha hung on to that — it seemed eminently sensible advice.

A rocket exploded with a ferocious bang, showering the night sky with flecks of gold and silver. She could hear the murmuring appreciation of the crowd gathered below. The baby slept on, oblivious. But how could she sleep through it? And after all their tip-toeing around!

When Barney returned home later, she was in bed, fast asleep. The baby lay awake, staring thoughtfully at the night sky.

"Sshh, baby," he whispered, lifting her gently. Cradling her carefully in his arms, he went downstairs to feed and change her and then sat on a

TORQUAY

Originally a fishing village, today Torquay is a glamorous, well-planned West Country resort. The harbour is always busy with boats, and the long beach is carefully kept and maintained.

Sub-tropical scrubs and palm trees flourish in the wonderful climate and the hillside gardens are floodlit at night in many different colours.

The town has historical connections, too. Napoleon, Napoleon III and Russian royalty all visited here, and the human bones that were found in Kent's Cavern proved man had existed far earlier than had first been thought!

© Pictor International.

while, slightly amazed to discover she'd dropped off again. They all had sleep to catch up on, it seemed.

Alysha didn't waken until long, blissful hours later. Barney was slumbering beside her, snoring gently.

She fumbled for the clock, slightly shocked to discover the night was nearly over. Barney must have seen to the baby then — bless him. She still felt tired; she supposed one good night wasn't going to change all that.

But lying in bed, listening to the silence, how content she was. Now, if only she could get this naming business sorted.

She heard the baby stir. By the time she'd fed and changed her and brought her back upstairs, light gleamed through the window. Holding the child gently, she pulled back the curtain.

There had been no frost. The sky was grey, as if the smoke from the huge bonfire still lingered. On the horizon, light was spreading, morning not far away.

"Beautiful, isn't it?" Barney appeared at her side,

Devon

tousle-headed and yawning. "I've always loved this time of morning. Let's face it, Alysha, it's a good job, too — we've seen enough of it this week."

Abruptly, she frowned, deep in thought.

"Dawn . . ." A slow shiver of delight travelled the length of her spine. "Dawn."

Her arms tightened around the child.

"What do you think, Barney?" She held her breath, fingers crossed. This had got to be something they both liked.

"Dawn?" He frowned, trying it out for size. The beginnings of a slow smile surfaced. She'd always loved his smile. "I think it's beautiful," he whispered. "It certainly beats Thingy!"

And Barney's mum had been so kind.

"Dawn Elizabeth," she said grandly, loving the sound of it. Barney's arms stole around her waist, and she leaned back against him.

It was perfect, somehow signifying the beginnings of their new life together. She smiled faintly. She was becoming sentimental. It came with being a parent, she supposed.

The light spread out across the sky. Somewhere, a bird began to sing. It felt rather like the calm after the storm — all those fireworks, and the baby deciding to sleep peacefully at last, despite it.

Alysha gazed down at her daughter's little wrinkled, screwed-up face. How beautiful she was, Dawn Elizabeth.

The naming of her had changed something. Already, she appeared to have grown a little, moved on to the next stage of her babyhood. It was all too precious to miss, every blissful moment of it . . . ■

Dunvegan Castle, Skye

FOR over 700 years, Dunvegan Castle has been home to the chief of the clan MacLeod. As with any great family over the centuries, many priceless artefacts have been handed on for posterity.

But the MacLeods' most treasured possession is without doubt the one displayed in a glass case in the castle drawing-room — the fragile remains of a thousand-year-old tattered silk banner called the Bratach Shith, or Fairy Flag.

A gift from MacLeod's wife, rumoured to be one of the fairies, it saved him in battle twice and brought victory to the MacLeods.

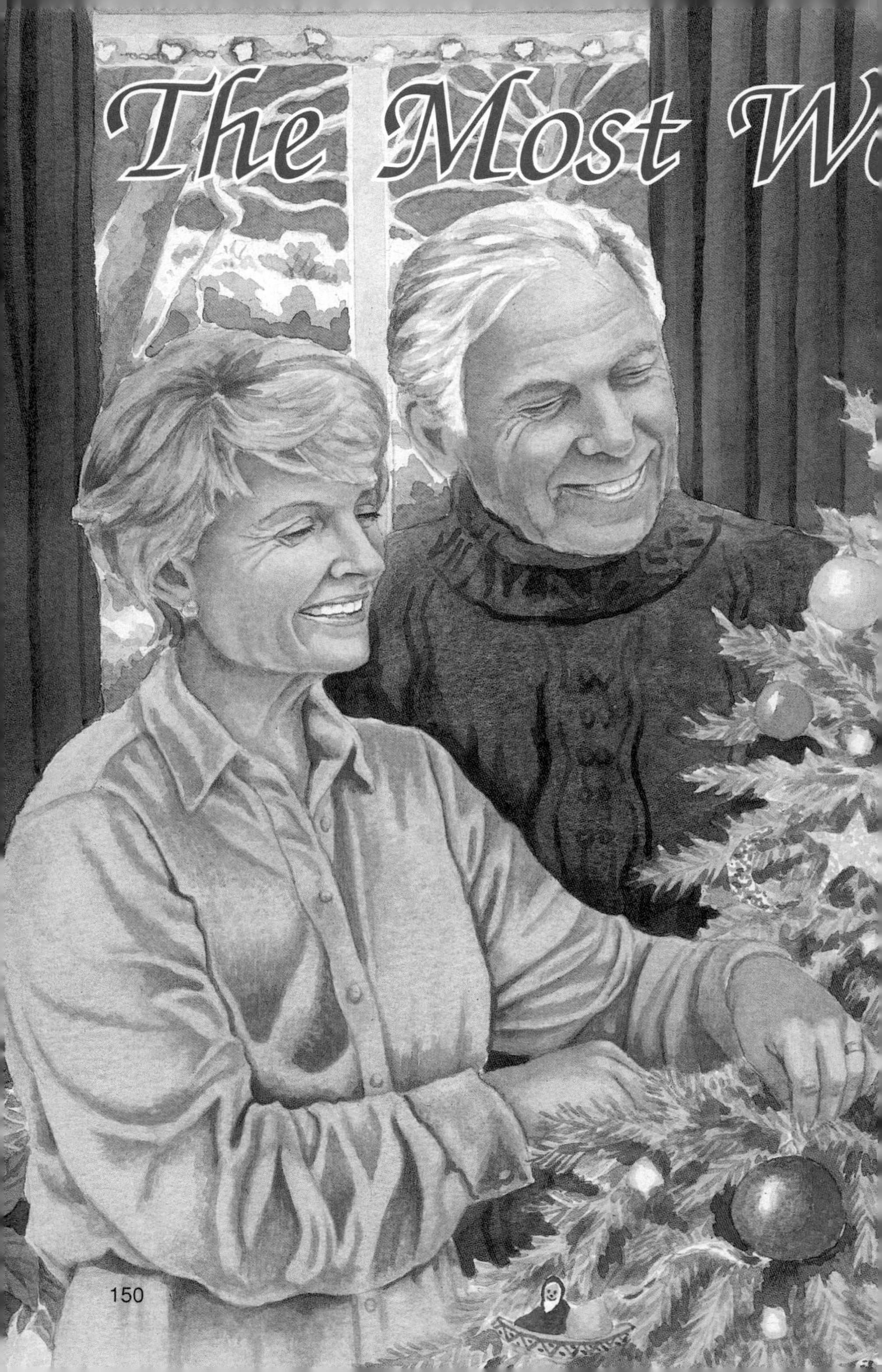

The Most W

derful Time Of The Year

by Sandy Simpson.

"JINGLE Bells" was playing on the radio. The air was rich with the smell of roasting turkey. The fairy lights on the Christmas tree were winking and sparkling cheerfully.

But Sheila Turner was in the depths of depression.

"Do you realise," she said mournfully to her husband, "this is our first Christmas in thirty-two years of marriage without Justin?"

"It's lovely and peaceful." Simon grinned mischievously.

"No, it isn't!" she wailed. "I miss him like mad."

"So do I." He pulled her close. "But maybe we should be thankful that we've had thirty-two great years. There are lots of families who never get together at Christmas."

Sheila leaned her head against his shoulder and nodded. She should be thankful. Still, it had come as a shock when their only son, Justin, had announced that his contract in Saudi had been extended and he wouldn't be home until January.

HE'D telephoned that morning to wish them a merry Christmas, but the line was muffled and he'd sounded so distant that his call had only increased Sheila's misery.

"The turkey smells great," Simon said, trying to cheer her up.

"It's too big. We'll never eat a fifteen pound turkey between the two of us . . . Oh, look! It's snowing!"

For a few moments, Sheila forgot about Justin as she hurried to the window. Tiny white snowflakes were falling from a slate grey sky and she felt a tingle of excitement as the spirit of Christmas touched her.

Illustration by Pat Gregory.

It was so beautiful. The garden and fields beyond were already dusted white, and it looked like a snowy scene from a Christmas card. In a very short time, all the children in the neighbourhood would be out sledging and having snowball fights . . .

"I love snow when we're both indoors, the house is cosy, and I don't have to travel to work," Simon said happily.

"It gives a magical feel to Christmas," Sheila agreed as the tiny flakes grew larger and larger.

A football suddenly came flying over the fence and narrowly missed their garden shed.

"Not again!" Sheila sighed. "That boy is a menace!"

"He's only having fun," Simon countered reasonably.

Sheila felt like throwing the football in the bin. She'd spoken only once to Gail Parish, their new neighbour. But she'd spoken on numerous occasions to Gail's son about his football landing in the garden.

"I'm tired of him asking for his ball back," she said, stomping through to the kitchen to baste the turkey.

"At least he asks, Sheila. There are plenty who would jump over the fence and rampage through the garden."

"Humbug," she muttered.

GAIL PARISH was so tired all she wanted to do was close her eyes and sleep for a hundred years.

Unfortunately, she had a turkey to cook, potatoes to peel, vegetables to prepare . . . And she'd promised her ten-year-old son that she would bake mince-pies. Garry loved mince-pies.

Removing the polythene from the turkey, she gave it a prod. It had defrosted. Thank goodness.

But before she could cook it, she had to find her roasting tin. It was in a box waiting to be unpacked. But which box?

Rummaging through a variety of bags and boxes in the narrow hallway, Gail fought to control her panic. Time was marching on. If she didn't find the tin, they would be lucky if they sat down to eat by ten o'clock tonight!

She must have been mad to have taken on the new post of Practice Nurse so close to Christmas. Not that she could have refused.

Compared to nursing part-time at the local infirmary, her new salary was great. And she now enjoyed a nine-to-five working day with every weekend off, which was fantastic after working shifts for so long.

But they'd had to move house. There had been Christmas shopping to deal with, carpets to be laid and curtains to hang.

And her parents had telephoned with the news that they wouldn't be hosting Christmas this year after all. They'd finally decided to make the once-in-a-lifetime visit to Aunty Peg in Canada. Would she manage without them?

Gail stifled a hysterical giggle when she found the roasting tin underneath a pile of dishes. Cope? She was a twenty-eight-year-old single parent. Of course she'd cope. Although she'd never cooked a Christmas dinner in her life . . .

"Something terrible has happened," Garry announced, throwing open the back door. "I kicked my ball over the fence again."

"Oh, Garry," she groaned.

WHEN they'd moved into the neighbourhood two weeks before, she and Garry had gone next door to introduce themselves. Mr Turner had been pleasant enough but his wife had eyed them with barely-concealed suspicion.

"Is it just the two of you?" she'd inquired.

"I'm afraid so." Gail had put a protective arm about her son. Although Jack Parish had walked out on them years ago, Garry was still sensitive about his father living abroad with his new family.

"I see," Mrs Turner said, with lips pursed.

"If you want your ball back," Gail said, washing the roasting tin in soapy water, "knock on the door and ask politely. They'll be fine."

"The last time I went round, Mrs Turner was grumpy. I don't like her."

"Don't say that," Gail chided gently. "Maybe you caught her in a bad mood. She's sure to be full of festive cheer today."

Garry didn't look convinced.

"I'm hungry."

"So am I," she said, picking up the cookery book.

"Is there any soup?"

"There will be once I've found my soup pot," Gail muttered, clearing a space on the work top.

"I'd really like a mince-pie."

"I'll make them the moment I've put the bird in the oven."

"Are we having roast potatoes?" Garry helped himself to crisps.

Gail was ashamed to admit she'd never roasted a potato in her life.

"Yes, we'll have roast potatoes," she promised rashly.

"And brussels sprouts?"

Gail gasped aloud. She'd forgotten to buy the sprouts!

"No stuffing. No sprouts." Garry shook his head sadly. "Well, at least you remembered the turkey."

Gail slumped on to a chair.

Mr Blobby was singing "Rudolph, the Red Nosed Reindeer" on the television amid riotous laughter from the studio audience. Their Christmas tree looked scrawny and bare, despite being covered in numerous decorations made from yoghurt cartons and egg boxes. Her parents were in Canada with Aunty Peg . . . And she had no sprouts.

"I'm really sorry!" Gail said, and burst into tears.

* * * *

"May I have my ball back, please?"

"Of course. In you come, lad, out of the snow." Simon ushered the boy into the hallway. "Are you having a nice Christmas?"

"It's OK, I suppose."

Simon was intrigued. The boy looked as if he had the weight of the world on his young shoulders.

"Was Santa good to you?"

Garry gave Simon an old-fashioned look.

"Mum's been a bit busy but I did get a Play Station."

Simon had never seen a Play Station but he guessed it must be a good present.

"Brilliant! Would you like a mince-pie? Or a slice of Christmas cake?"

"Yes, please." Garry visibly perked up. He smiled shyly at Sheila as they went into the kitchen.

"Merry Christmas, Mrs Turner."

"And to you," she said, but she frowned when she saw he'd brought snow in on his boots.

"What a lovely smell, Mrs Turner!" Garry's nostrils flared.

"Thank you, Garry." Despite the melting snow on the clean floor, her lips twitched.

"Fantastic mince-pies," he went on, wolfing down two in quick succession. "The best I've ever tasted."

IF he was trying to improve neighbourly relations, Simon thought to himself, it was working.

"My son tells me I make the best mince-pies in the world." Sheila smiled warmly.

"What age is he?" the boy asked, watching her wrap bacon round chipolata sausages.

"Justin is thirty-one. And he works abroad most of the time. This is the first time he's missed coming home for Christmas."

Garry was now picking the marzipan from a slice of home-made cake, and he looked up at Sheila with a sad smile.

"This is the first time we haven't spent Christmas with Gran and Grandad. They're away to Canada."

Sheila was surprised. She had assumed her neighbours would be spending the day with family and friends in their new home.

"I expect your mum is busy cooking your dinner," she said, noting that

Grandparents

KATE and Joe have now moved on
And reached another stage;
With quite a few grandchildren
They're at a mellow age.

They're very happy on their own
But overjoyed to be
A most important part of life
For their family.

The children come to visit
With offspring large and small
And Kate and Joe draw comfort from
The presence of them all.

What merriment they all enjoy
When everyone is there!
With games of cricket on the lawn
And other joys to share.

– Alice Drury.

his hair was shiny and blond and he had freckles on his nose. He reminded her a little of Justin at the same age.

"Sort of." Garry gave a funny little shrug. "She forgot to buy the sprouts and the stuffing. And I think she forgot the sausages as well."

"As long as she's remembered the turkey, eh?" Sheila hid her smile.

He nodded and sighed deeply.

"Mum's been busy with her new job. We still haven't unpacked all our stuff, so I'm not sure if we'll get soup because she can't find her soup pot. And Mum's hopeless at making gravy and I can't remember her ever making roast potatoes before. Gran always cooks Christmas dinner."

He looked so disgruntled Sheila was finding it difficult not to laugh.

"I'm sure your mum will make a great dinner," she said, winking at Simon as he returned with the missing football.

"I dunno." Garry rubbed his forehead. "She was crying when I left."

Sheila stopped what she was doing and wiped her hands on her apron. She didn't want to be nosy but she didn't like to think of the young woman next door sitting alone and crying. Not on Christmas Day.

"Would you like to see my son's train set?" Simon put an arm about the boy. "I've started to set it up in the spare room."

"And help yourself to another mince-pie, dear."

There was a large puddle of melted snow and pie crumbs beside the table but she ignored the mess. She couldn't stop thinking about Garry's mother. It was little wonder she'd forgotten the sprouts and the stuffing when she'd just moved house and started a new job.

It must be difficult coping without any support.

TWO minutes later, Sheila headed next door and rang the bell. She might regret this, but she couldn't live with herself if she didn't at least extend the invitation.

"Oh, hello." Gail looked startled. "I hope Garry isn't bothering you."

"Not at all." Sheila was overwhelmed with concern when she saw Gail's red eyes. "He's helping Simon set up my son's old train set."

"He'll love that." Gail hesitated. "Would you like to come in?"

Sheila stepped inside and shivered. The house felt cold. There were no delicious smells floating through from the kitchen. And there were boxes and bags everywhere.

"I see you're still unpacking," she commented.

"It's amazing the junk that one person and one small boy can accumulate." Gail pulled a face.

"Garry tells me your parents are away."

Gail nodded and swallowed.

"I hope you don't think I'm speaking out of turn," Sheila rushed on, "but we usually have our son with us at Christmas but he couldn't get

156

home this year. I was wondering if you and Garry would like to help us eat our turkey. It's enormous."

Gail's eyes widened, then two huge tears spilled down her cheeks.

"Oh, thank you, Mrs Turner," she breathed.

"Call me, Sheila, dear . . ."

"Sheila," Gail said shakily. "We would love to join you."

"Good. We'll see you next door when you're ready."

* * * *

"That was wonderful," Gail enthused, laying her knife and fork on her empty plate. "I wish I could cook like that."

"It was great," Garry added, patting his full stomach. "If we'd been at home, there wouldn't have been any sprouts or sausages or stuffing —"

"Or perfectly cooked roast potatoes and gravy." Gail laughed, thanking Simon as he replenished her wine glass.

"Creating a Christmas dinner isn't difficult," Sheila demurred. "If you hadn't just moved and started a new job, you'd have coped brilliantly."

"Maybe . . ." Gail giggled.

They decided to wait a short while before the Christmas pudding, and Gail heard all about the Turners' son, Justin.

He'd graduated with honours in civil engineering and had worked all over the country designing roads and bridges before moving abroad.

"It's great that everyone can travel the world so easily," Gail said. "But sometimes it can make for a lonely Christmas."

"My dad works abroad," Garry spoke up proudly. "He lives in France."

Gail flushed. It was good that Garry liked to talk about his father, but she'd rather he hadn't spoken about him in front of the neighbours.

"Would you like to help me serve the pudding?" Sheila asked tactfully.

Gail gave her a grateful smile and followed her into the kitchen.

"Garry misses his dad." Gail sighed.

"I can imagine. Is there much contact?"

Gail shook his head.

"My husband was offered a teaching job in France when Garry was a baby. He left to find us a house and get everything settled. Unfortunately, he found the love of his life instead."

"Poor you," Sheila said gently. "Poor Garry."

"We're OK." Gail shrugged.

"He's a grand wee lad. You've done a good job with him." Sheila laughed suddenly. "Even if he does drive me wild with that football."

The two women were still laughing when they soaked the pudding with warmed brandy and set it alight. Gail couldn't believe they had forged such an easy friendship in so short a time.

"What a pudding!" Simon roared, clapping his hands with delight .

"Won't it set our mouths on fire?" Garry asked, watching the blue flames dance around the plate.

Then the door opened suddenly and a tall man carrying a bag filled with gaily wrapped parcels stood smiling at them.

"Merry Christmas, everyone!"

"Justin!" Sheila forgot the flaming pudding as she ran to greet her son.

"Welcome home, lad." Simon embraced him warmly.

Gail didn't want to stare, but Justin Turner was gazing at her over his father's shoulder. He was oddly familiar and heart-stoppingly attractive and it struck her that he had the kindest brown eyes she had ever seen . . .

Later, Sheila hummed to herself as she prepared turkey sandwiches for supper. She doubted if anyone was hungry, but it was traditional!

She could hear Simon and Garry making silly woo woo noises as they played with the train. Gail and Justin were talking quietly in the lounge.

Wiping the steam from the window, she looked out on to a winter wonderland. In the darkness, the glow from the street lamps had turned the snow to orange. Sheila could just make out the strains of "Silent Night" as the lady in the house opposite played her piano.

IT had been a wonderful Christmas. The day might have started badly, but with each passing hour it had got better and better! They had made two wonderful new friends from next door. And Justin was back to stay.

When he telephoned that morning, he'd actually been in London having flown in the previous evening. The Saudi contract was finished and he was due to start a three-year contract at home after the new year.

It was the best Christmas present he could have given her.

Popping her head round the lounge door, Sheila was about to ask if anyone wanted coffee. But something stopped her.

Their neighbour's piano could be heard tinkling softly in the background and the log fire was crackling in the grate. Justin and Gail were sitting very close together on the sofa. Maybe she was jumping to conclusions, but she had a funny feeling that Christmas might be weaving its own particular brand of magic between her son and her new friend.

Tiptoeing back into the kitchen, she felt a rush of happiness. This was what Christmas was about. Families and friends, love and togetherness.

"You're looking rather pleased with yourself," Simon commented, arranging some mince-pies on a plate for Garry.

"I'm feeling very pleased with myself!" She laughed.

Setting aside the plate, Simon pulled her into his arms and positioned her underneath the mistletoe.

"It's been a great Christmas," he said.

"The best ever," she corrected, and reached up on tiptoe for his kiss. ■

Illustration by Klim Forster.

Rolling Back The Years

by Barbara Povey.

S ISTER MCARDLE walked purposefully the length of the ward to stare at the sprig of mistletoe tied with a red ribbon to Bertha Thomas's wispy top-knot.

"Who did that?"

Bertha's face assumed its most uncomprehending expression, and Jane McArdle, with an exasperated "tut", marched back to the nursing station.

She didn't really need an answer. She knew the culprit would be Student Nurse Oliver. A scatty girl, if ever there was one, head full of nonsense.

She was always chattering. The

ward was never quiet when she was about. And the laughter she encouraged from the elderly ladies with her silly jokes . . . !

"Where's Oliver?" she asked Staff Nurse Lomax.

"Collecting a patient from Orthopaedic, Sister," Staff replied.

"Are you coming to the party tonight?" she added, in a vain attempt to divert Sister's attention from the unlucky student.

"I think not. When Oliver returns I want to see her." Sister disappeared into her office, closing the door so swiftly that the silver Christmas bells tinkled in the draught.

"What's the matter now, Staff?" Nurse Keane glanced towards the office.

"It's Oliver again — she just can't get on with Sister. Clash of personalities, I suppose."

"Well, she does seem to ask for trouble," Nurse Keane agreed. "But she has the makings of a good nurse — the patients are always happy when she's on the ward.

"And it is Christmas Eve!"

"Perhaps Sister won't be too hard on her this time."

JANE MCARDLE stood at her office window, looking out at the view she knew so well.

That headache was back — she must try to relax. She needed a holiday, but with staff shortages that was out of the question.

Sensing, rather than actually hearing, a rustle outside her door, she anticipated the hesitant knock, and sat behind her desk.

"Staff said you wanted to see me, Sister."

Nurse Oliver had a bright, attractive face and eyes which, even in the present circumstances, managed to sparkle.

Jane McArdle took a deep breath . . . and then paused. She seemed to spend so much of her time these days finding fault . . . but the patients should come first.

"The patient from Orthopaedic. Is she comfortable?"

Nurse Oliver was clearly taken by surprise.

"Er . . . yes, Sister. Ariadne Robinson — fractured neck of femur — successfully pinned." She finished on a confident note.

"Hm. Well, we'll see."

Sister rose from her desk, motioning Nurse Oliver to accompany her.

All the while, her mind toyed with the name. Ariadne? Could it be *the* Ariadne?

As they approached the new patient's bed, Jane McArdle knew, without a doubt, she had seen that face before.

Pale skin stretched over high cheekbones, and though the hair was now silver, there was no shadow of a doubt. This was Ariadne!

160

Ariadne, after all this time. Goodness, she must be nearly ninety.

Twenty years ago, she had looked such a delicate woman, but she was tough.

In her youth, she'd once revealed, her father had had a stall in the fish market. All those years of standing on cold flagged floors, yelling "Finnan haddock", "Fresh mackerel," or "Buy your pint of shrimps here", had made her into a survivor.

Patients and nurses alike soon came to terms with her tough inner core.

Arry, as she preferred to be called, was the ringleader in any prank in those days, to the delight of the students and the vexation of Sister Nelson.

Horatio, they'd called Sister — but she'd never turned a blind eye!

And now, Sister McArdle thought, Ariadne is my responsibility . . .

"Hello, Ariadne! How do you feel?" Jane smiled her professional smile.

Faded blue eyes looked up at her with a slightly puzzled expression, then suddenly cleared.

"Good gracious, McArdle! Are you still here?" Ariadne glanced at Sister's dark blue dress.

"You made the grade, then?"

FOR Jane, the years slipped away. Her dark blue dress became the white uniform of a student nurse.

Christmas Eve in Women's Geriatrics, with Rosie, Gina and the irrepressible Kath . . .

She felt again the ever-present anxiety, prompted by a healthy respect for Sister Nelson, awareness of her own lack of skill, and that genuine desire to ease the suffering of the people in her care.

Jane had made up her mind by the age of nine to become a nurse. Long hours, hard work and low pay had not weakened that desire.

The ward was bright that year with paper chains and baubles. Cards provided a frieze of colour behind each bed, and a bunch of mistletoe dangled optimistically from the centre light.

It had been a busy morning — a catastrophic morning.

Horatio, otherwise Sister, had ordered all dentures to be cleaned and sterilised.

Following a suggestion of Ariadne's, Kath and Gina attempted to hasten the task by collecting teeth from all the patients. Then they realised redistribution would be a bit like Dandini and the glass slipper.

The inevitable happened. One set of sparkling clean dentures remained in the white enamel bowl — and Maggie O'Callaghan was definitely not Cinderella.

Panic stations!

They sorted it out in the nick of time.

Horatio never knew of the dilemma, or the students would not have been entrusted with escorting four patients into town to view the Christmas lights.

These four ladies had responded well to treatment, but had no relatives to care for them.

They were stuck on the ward until provision could be made — which would definitely not be over the holidays.

It was then Horatio proved she had a heart beating beneath that dark blue dress. She decided that her first-year students should wheel these patients into town to soak up the atmosphere.

"But, remember, you must be back here by four. It will be growing dark by then. Do you understand?"

"Yes, Sister," they chorused.

An afternoon away from St Bridget's! They couldn't believe their luck.

THE four ladies were wrapped up warmly, red blankets tucked around their legs, and the girls donned their dark blue uniform coats.

They made a colourful procession as they set off down the drive.

"Wagons roll!" Ariadne cried.

The town was a heaving mass of good-humoured last-minute shoppers, and the group from St Bridget's were in high spirits. Streets were bright with coloured lights, and in the town square a huge Christmas tree glowed.

Edna, Maggie, Dora and Arry "ooohed" and "aaahed" their appreciation.

The mills had closed down for the holiday, and mill girls, linking arms across the pavement, sang "Rudolph, The Red-nosed Reindeer".

The excitement was infectious — but daylight was already fading.

They were on their way back to St Bridget's when it happened . . .

The Drum & Monkey in Bridge Street was full to overflowing. Jolly customers spilled from the bright interior.

Men in overalls with pints of beer in their hands . . . office workers enjoying a gin and tonic before their homeward journey . . . everywhere, the golden glow of happiness.

The wheelchair procession struggled along the crowded pavement, Kath in the lead.

"Make way, please!" she shouted.

"'Course, luv," a big burly man answered, "but what's your hurry? Let's buy you a Christmas drink."

"Sorry! No can do." Kath grinned at him. "We're on duty."

"Hey, but what about Grandma?" the big fellow persisted. "How about

Balquhidder, Perthshire

TAKE a gentle stroll through bonnie Strathyre and you'll come upon the picturesque village of Balquhidder in Perthshire, famous for being the final resting place of the legendary folk hero, Rob Roy MacGregor. His grave at Balquhidder bears the inscription "MacGregor, despite them".

Balquhidder was actually the home of the MacLarens. They can trace their roots back to when they were given land there, and in Strathearn, by King Kenneth MacAlpin in AD 843.

The MacLarens and the MacGregors were in fact notorious rivals — and sometimes deadly enemies!

BALQUHIDDER, PERTHSHIRE: J CAMPBELL KERR.

a drop of rum, Ma, just to keep out the cold?"

If it hadn't been Kath and Arry in the lead, that might have been the end of it. But Kath, with her merry green eyes and unruly curls, was always devil-may-care, and Arry had never refused the offer of a drink in her life.

In no time at all, she had a small glass of rum in her hand. The pub's regulars, generous with Christmas spirit and picturing their own grandmothers in the wheelchairs, produced port and lemon for Edna and Dora and a sweet sherry for Maggie.

"Now what will the Angels of Mercy have?" a voice from the bar shouted — but there the students drew the line.

They never noticed the photographer from the local paper. Luckily, he came on the scene after the last drops of "medicine" had been drunk.

"Just one picture for the Christmas issue, girls," he pleaded. Before they could protest, a bulb flashed and he was gone.

The first strains of "Away In A Manger" arose from the tap room, and everyone joined in. As the voices swelled, underpinning all the rest was Ariadne's clear, strong contralto.

AFTER an impromptu carol service, they returned to the hospital at full gallop. Gina distributed mints to disguise any lingering suggestion of alcohol.

Their luck held. As they entered the ward, rosy cheeked and out of breath, Horatio was just consulting her watch.

"Four o'clock precisely! Well done, nurses. I hope everyone has behaved in a manner befitting St Bridget's."

They smiled demurely.

The picture appeared in the paper's special edition, but as the caption merely said *St Bridget's Angels*, Horatio contented herself with a disapproving glare and something that sounded like "Hrrumph!"

It was, after all, Christmas Eve.

Unfortunately, Jane's mother quizzed her about the photograph and how they happened to be in front of the Drum & Monkey.

Then the storm broke.

"Oh, Jane, how could you? Those senior citizens were in your charge. Had you no respect for their dignity?"

Jane opened her mouth to protest, but her mother was in full flow.

"And Arry, as you call her — why, with a name like Ariadne she might well be from the aristocracy." Mother breathed the word in a reverent way.

Jane burst out laughing.

"Honestly, Mum, have you heard yourself? Aristocracy! If you only knew.

"And if Arry is an aristocrat, so what? She's stuck in hospital over Christmas, just like Edna, Dora and Maggie. They deserve some pleasure."

But her mother's words had planted a germ of doubt in Jane's mind. Had they offended the patients in their charge on that merry day in town?

It was a small doubt, but through the years, it had festered whenever the memory of the Christmas outing came back to haunt her . . .

GAZING down at the slight form of Ariadne Robinson, Sister McArdle recalled her partners in that Christmas Eve escapade . . . Rose was happily married and raising a brood of children on a dairy farm in Cheshire.

The stunningly attractive Gina had been snapped up by a young houseman, who eventually became a GP, and was now his wife, receptionist and nurse.

And Kath, the maddest of all . . . Each Christmas, Jane received a letter from Kath, telling her all about life in the missionary hospital in Africa, where she'd found her true vocation.

Her ready smile and cheery disposition were worth more than gold in that isolated outpost.

"Daydreaming, McArdle? What would Sister Nelson have to say about that?"

Ariadne's words might be sharp, but her tone was not. A hint of the old mischief appeared in her pale eyes.

"I knew you'd make it. You were a born nurse."

Her words were solace to Jane's troubled mind — but it was all so long ago. Ariadne had aged. Perhaps she didn't remember.

"You really thought I would make the grade — after that Christmas Eve? The picture in the paper — everything?"

"Sister McArdle, that Christmas was the best I ever had. So much kindness and so much happiness.

"Yes! Without a doubt. The very best Christmas I ever had."

The old lady smiled up at Jane, a contented smile. Then she closed her eyes and drifted off into a peaceful, healing sleep.

Sister smiled, too, at the probationer by her side.

"Get off for your tea now, Nurse Oliver," she said.

The little matter of the mistletoe in Bertha Thomas's hair had lost its importance. Hadn't she been remarkably like Nurse Oliver in her student days? Yet Ariadne had believed her to be a born nurse, even then.

As she walked back to the nursing station, Jane realised her headache had disappeared.

"What time is that party tonight?" she asked Staff with a grin.

After all, it *was* Christmas Eve! ∎

THE ringing of the telephone woke Ellie. Her first thought was Heather. It must be the baby!

by Sheila Lewis.

Abandoning slippers and dressing-gown, she ran to the phone and snatched up the receiver.

"Andrew?"

"Yes, Ellie, it's me," her son-in-law answered, his voice sounding a little strained. "We're at the hospital. Heather's pains started in the night, but the doctor says it will be some time yet before the baby comes. She said you wanted to know as soon as possible."

"Yes, yes, I did. I do!" Nervous excitement was making Ellie confused.

"You can come along to the hospital if you like," Andrew went on. "It could be a long wait, though . . ."

There was something in his voice that made her think that perhaps he and Heather wanted her there.

"I wouldn't be in the way, would I?" she asked, knowing that sitting at home alone would be agonising now.

"No, not at all!" Andrew sounded relieved. "I'll

Friends In

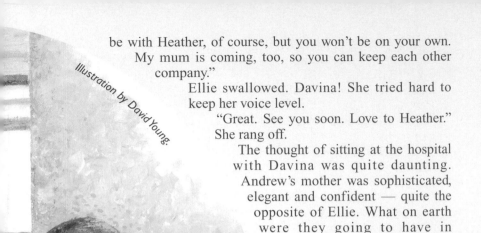

Illustration by David Young.

be with Heather, of course, but you won't be on your own. My mum is coming, too, so you can keep each other company."

Ellie swallowed. Davina! She tried hard to keep her voice level.

"Great. See you soon. Love to Heather." She rang off.

The thought of sitting at the hospital with Davina was quite daunting. Andrew's mother was sophisticated, elegant and confident — quite the opposite of Ellie. What on earth were they going to have in common to chat about?

Oh, what did it matter what they chatted about? Ellie shook herself, annoyed at the silliness of her thoughts. None of that mattered today. Not on the day her first grandchild was due to be born!

SHE began to rush about and then stopped herself, remembering Andrew's warning that it could be a long wait. No need to get into a panic, she thought.

Just get dressed, have something to eat, then make for the hospital. Thank goodness it was Sunday and she didn't need to open the shop.

Swinging open the wardrobe, she froze in her tracks. What would she wear? After all, she would be meeting Davina. She had to think carefully about what she put on. Andrew's mother would be wearing something chic and elegant, and Ellie didn't want to let Heather down.

It was then that a hysterical giggle rose up in her throat. What was she thinking of?

Waiting

167

This was the birth of their first grandchild, for both mothers. What kind of dress code could there possibly be for that?

She left the house barely ten minutes later, with only a cup of tea for breakfast. She was too excited to eat. She was wearing her black trouser suit and stripy blouse, one of her own creations.

Her car, which had a tendency to sulk on occasion, started first time. Mind you, it was old, if not indeed elderly, but it was the first car she'd ever owned and she'd had to pass her driving test last year before buying it.

No doubt Davina would arrive in her expensive car. Nothing but the best for her. She remembered Heather once saying that Davina only wore designer labels.

"Pretty draughty," Ellie had said jokingly.

"Oh, Mum." Heather had hugged her. "It's just the way she is. Your clothes are every bit as fashionable and trendy."

ELLIE doubted that, but knew Heather was trying to comfort her, to boost her confidence. The wedding had been only two months away then and she'd been sewing like mad, making the wedding dress, the bridesmaids' dresses and, last of all, her own outfit.

Ellie dragged her thoughts away from the wedding and back to the present. She joined the slip road for the motorway and eased the car into the correct lane. My goodness, I'm getting better all the time, she thought.

What would Bill have thought about her driving her own car? It was odd, but when anything new happened in her life, she always wondered what Bill would have thought. Now, their first grandchild was nearly here!

She bit her lip. Bill hadn't lived to see their own child born. Ellie had been widowed when she was eight months pregnant.

She recalled Heather's wedding day again. How proud Bill would have been of their daughter then. And he would have loved Andrew just as much as I do, she thought.

He was a kind boy. She'd known the first time she'd set eyes on him that he was right for Heather. As right as Bill had been for her.

Bill would have been at ease with Ted and Davina Hepburn, too. They were a nice couple really, and she knew it just was her own shyness and lack of confidence that made her stay in the background.

Naturally, she had never told Heather all this, but her daughter was a perceptive girl and Ellie suspected that she knew most of it anyway.

She'd reached another slip road, this time off the motorway. The hospital was only a mile or so away now. She realised she had been deliberately going over past memories as a way of shutting out her worries about Heather.

She hoped with all her heart that she'd be all right. Ellie remembered the long hours of her own labour. Thank goodness Andrew would be with Heather to support her, but she was still anxious.

The hospital sign loomed into view and Ellie indicated she was turning off the road. The carpark had one or two empty spaces near the entrance and she parked beside a gleaming gold car that she recognised immediately as Davina's.

S HE found the maternity ward after a few wrong turns and was directed to the waiting room, where Davina sat all on her own. To her surprise, the other woman rushed over and hugged her.

"Ellie, I'm so glad to see you!" Davina's voice was high with anxiety.

"Has something happened? Is everything all right?" Ellie felt her stomach somersault and her knees weaken.

"Oh, yes, everything's fine! Sorry, I didn't mean to frighten you." Davina took her arm and led her to a chair. "Andrew was in here just a moment ago. Things are going well, but slowly."

Ellie sat down, the flutters of panic subsiding.

"It's me," Davina said. "I get in such a state when I'm on my own. My imagination goes into overdrive."

"Didn't Ted come with you?" Ellie asked.

Davina shook her head.

"He's in Singapore on business. Isn't that typical? Did you eat breakfast before you left the house?"

"Er, no," Ellie replied, surprised at the sudden change of conversation.

"I'm dying for a bacon roll," Davina said. "I'll go and see if I can find some."

Ellie almost choked. Davina Hepburn eating a bacon roll?

For a stunned second she watched as Davina left the waiting-room. Her trouser suit was blue, worn with a red T-shirt. Very elegant, but . . . something was not quite right about the total ensemble. Ellie couldn't quite put a finger on it.

The waiting room door swung open again and Andrew entered.

"Ellie! I'm so glad you're here." He hugged her fiercely.

"How is she, Andrew?" Ellie could hear the note of panic in her own voice.

"She's fine. Fed up it's taking so long. She wanted me to ask you how long you were in labour with her."

"It doesn't matter how long." Ellie skilfully evaded the question. "Tell her it's worth it, and the important thing is to listen to what the doctor and midwives tell her."

Andrew nodded and then turned and headed for the door.

"I'll tell her that. I'd better get back now. I don't want to leave her on her own . . ."

At least Heather had Andrew at her side, Ellie thought to herself. Her own labour had been very long and lonely without Bill being there for her.

DAVINA reappeared then, pushing open the waiting-room door with her foot and holding a cardboard box in her hands. The tantalising smell of bacon and coffee was almost overpowering.

"Where did you get them?" Ellie smiled. "Is the cafeteria open this early?"

"No, but I know this little place round the corner. The only problem is the nurse said we can't eat in here. How about nipping along the corridor to the stairway? It's either that or we head for the carpark!"

Somewhat bemused, Ellie found herself sitting on the top step of the second-floor stairway, eating a delicious bacon roll alongside her daughter's mother-in-law.

"I do envy you, you know," Davina said, nearly causing Ellie to scald her tongue with surprise.

"Envy me?" Ellie was amazed.

"Mmm." Davina wiped a trickle of melted butter from her chin. "You're always so calm and clever. I'm just a mass of nerves and indecision when Ted's not around."

"But I'm not like that at all," Ellie protested.

"Don't deny it, Ellie. I've admired you since the day we met. I could never have brought up Andrew on my own as you did Heather. Nor could I have made as good a job of it. Heather's a real credit to you."

"It wasn't easy," Ellie murmured.

"No, but you did it, and you made it. You have a fine daughter. I'm so proud that Andrew married her."

By now, Ellie was speechless. There was no doubt in her mind that Davina was sincere.

"And then the wedding. You sailed through that, having made all those wonderful dresses and outfits," Davina said. "Everyone thought Heather's dress was by some posh new designer!"

It was time to confess, Ellie decided.

"I thought I would meet myself coming back sometimes, in the build-up to the wedding," she said, knowing Davina would understand what she meant. "All I could think about was the elegant Hepburns dressed in the best and our side in home-made frocks."

Davina giggled.

"Elegant dresses don't mean much when you just hand over a bit of plastic for them. You created your outfits. And look what happened after

Retirement

KATE and Joe have settled down
To peaceful autumn days.
Retirement is a time of rest;
A calm and gentle phase.

Although their steps are slower now
They're fit and active, too;
With many happy years ahead
And living yet to do.

They're still the very best of friends
Content in every way
So glad to have each other
As they go from day to day.

But best of all, at eventide
They sit by the firelight's glow –
And reminisce about the past
And the days of long ago.

– *Alice Drury.*

the wedding!"

Ellie smiled. It had been a new beginning for her as well as Heather and Andrew.

She'd received so many commissions from guests at the wedding who'd admired her dressmaking skills that she'd been able to rent a small shop. In the two years since, custom had grown so much that she was supplying fabrics and trimmings for other dressmakers. And she had been able to buy a car!

Whoever would have believed that a hobby she loved would turn out to be a career? Bill would've been so proud.

As proud as he'd been when she'd walked down the aisle in the wedding dress she'd made all those years ago for herself.

How she still missed him. And how cruel it was that a tragic accident should have robbed her daughter of a father and this new baby of a loving grandfather . . .

Life just wasn't fair sometimes, she mused. But please let everything turn out all right for Heather and Andrew. That really would be too much to bear.

SUDDENLY, a door behind them opened. A young nurse stood there, smiling.

"Oh, there you are! Mr Hepburn asked me to find you and tell you that the midwife thinks everything will go quite quickly now. Heather's doing really well and the baby's heartbeat is strong and regular."

Instinctively, Ellie and Davina turned to each other and clasped hands.

Back in the waiting-room they sat close together, united in their anticipation and concern for a safe delivery. They talked a little as time went by and Ellie found she was glad that Davina was there with her.

They never knew exactly how long it was before Andrew joined them, eyes suspiciously wet, but a grin from ear to ear on his delighted face.

"A girl . . . we have a daughter! And she's absolutely beautiful — just like her mother. They're both fine — it's me who's in a state!"

Davina immediately burst into tears, while Ellie's eyes were wet, too, as she released all the tension, giving thanks for the safe delivery. They both moved to hug Andrew at the same time, ending up in a three-way group hug with many tears and lots of laughter.

They followed him to the ward then, tiptoeing in to see their new granddaughter.

Heather was sitting up in bed, looking tired but radiant, the baby nestling in her arms.

Ellie gave her a daughter a kiss, then a long look and, satisfied that all was well, bent over to gaze at the baby. On the other side of the bed, Davina was doing exactly the same.

Neither remembered exactly what they said, but each could describe the baby in minute detail. They took turns to hold the new arrival, Davina insisting that Ellie held her first.

Finally, reassured that all was well, they handed over the baby to Andrew and left the new family to rest. Davina reminded Andrew to phone his father and Ellie's last thought as she left the ward was that Bill would have been so proud!

"I just can't go home to an empty house, Ellie," Davina said outside the hospital doors. "Let's go and have a coffee."

They sat in a nearby café and talked about the baby for a while, making plans to buy clothes, baby-sit, go for walks with the pram.

"Maybe we could do all these things together?" Davina suggested.

Ellie realised that she'd been completely wrong about Davina. She wasn't distant at all. In fact, she seemed to be a little lonely. Her elegant, confident poise was obviously a front that people who didn't know her very well couldn't see past.

"Yes, I'd like that," she said.

"You know, Ellie, it's a new beginning for more than the baby today," Davina said. "It's us, too. We're going to be good friends now, aren't we?"

"Yes, and I'm so pleased. I have to confess I was a little apprehensive about meeting you again," Ellie said.

"I was so excited that I couldn't decide what to wear! Knowing you'd be so smart, I ended up changing a couple of times." Davina laughed.

And it was then that Ellie suddenly realised what was so odd about Davina's ensemble.

"That would explain your ear-rings," she said with a smile.

Davina put her hands up to her ears and removed the offending ear-rings. To her amazement, one was bright blue and the other emerald green!

Seconds later, their waitress turned to the coffee shop manageress.

"Do you think those two ladies are all right?" she asked, nodding towards Ellie and Davina, who were laughing and crying helplessly.

"Oh, yes," was the reply. "They're just good friends having a laugh together!" ■

Printed and Published in Great Britain by D.C. Thomson & Co., Ltd., Dundee, Glasgow and London.
© D.C. Thomson & Co., 2003. While every reasonable care will be taken, neither D.C. Thomson, Ltd., nor its agents will accept liability for loss or damage to colour transparencies or any other material submitted to this publication.
ISBN 0-85116-832-9
EAN 9-780851-168326

ST ANDREWS: J CAMPBELL KERR.

174